Beryl Bainbridge

Mum and Mr Armitage

and other stories

Flamingo
Published by Fontana Paperbacks

First published by
Gerald Duckworth & Co. Ltd 1985

This Flamingo edition first published
in 1987 by Fontana Paperbacks,
8 Grafton Street, London W1X 3LA

Flamingo is an imprint of
Fontana Paperbacks, part of
the Collins Publishing Group

Made and printed in Great Britain by
William Collins Sons & Co. Ltd, Glasgow

Mum and Mr Armitage

Beryl Bainbridge was born in the 1930s in Liverpool and spent her early working years there as a juvenile character actress in repertory. She started writing seriously when she left the theatre behind to have her first baby.

She has written many highly-praised novels, including *The Dressmaker*, which was runner-up for the Booker Prize, and *The Bottle Factory Outing*, also a Booker Prize runner-up and winner of the *Guardian* fiction prize. *Injury Time* won the Whitbread Award in 1977. She also writes for television. *English Journey* was a BBC television series.

Beryl Bainbridge now lives in Camden Town, London, in a house full of Victorian bric-a-brac and old photographs, which she collects.

Also by Beryl Bainbridge

Harriet said . . .
The Dressmaker
The Bottle Factory Outing
Sweet William
A Quiet Life
Injury Time
Young Adolf
Another Part of the Wood
Winter Garden
A Weekend with Claude
English Journey (travel)
Watson's Apology

Contents

For Charlie and Bertie Russell

1
Mum and Mr Armitage

Being elderly, Miss Emmet, the thin lady from the Midlands, expected to be left out of things. And she was. Some of the younger guests – Walter Hood for instance, whose mother had recently died, and the girl who had served in the Land Army during the war and was wearing a halter-top in spite of the weather – took it badly.

'I think it's downright rude,' the girl said, when for the third evening on the trot the regular crowd went off into the library to play cards, jamming their chairs so tightly against the door that it was impossible for anyone else to join them.

'I've never even set foot in the library,' complained Walter Hood. 'They're in there every blessed minute.'

Thinking that six shelves stacked with detective novels hardly constituted a library, Miss Emmet said Goodnight and went up to her room. But for the smoke that billowed out from the hearth as she closed the door the young people would scarcely have noticed she was gone.

'Perhaps things will get better when Mum and Mr Armitage arrive,' the land-girl said. She felt brighter just mentioning their names.

The regular crowd who frequented the Herbert Arms Hotel

Christmas, Easter and summer never stopped talking among themselves about Mum and Mr Armitage. What good sports they were! What fun they were to be with! Life hummed when Mum was in the vicinity. Her real name was Rosemary Mumford, but nobody ever called her that. At least, not after she became a widow. In the middle of the war she had received one of those telegrams regretting that her husband was missing, believed killed. He had last been seen above Düsseldorf, baling out of a blazing Wellington bomber. It was thought that he and Mum had spent their honeymoon at the hotel, in No.4, the big room at the front with the brass bed by the window and the stuffed stoat on the mantelpiece. They had returned again the following year, in summer. Mum had known the area as a child; her uncle, it was said, had been in charge of the mine over at Marton. When she was little Mum had gone down the mine with a candle attached to her helmet.

The stoat had been ensconced in the front bedroom for the last ten years, out of consideration for Mum's feelings. It had previously stood, impaled on a stick on a bed of withered bracken and encased in glass, on the window-sill in the library, until, the Christmas after she had received the telegram, Mum had knocked the case to the ground, shattering the glass. It was assumed it was not an accident. Bits of stuffing had come out of the stoat and Mr White had hidden it out of sight in the front bedroom so as not to cause Mum further aggravation. It obviously reminded her of her husband.

There was even talk that Mum had undergone one of those breakdowns peculiar to arty types, that she had actually been put into hospital; although some argued that it was more physical than mental, or rather that something had happened, while her mind was temporarily distracted with grief, which had resulted in an injury. What sort of injury, no one could say. It was all very much a matter of conjecture, and so long ago.

That she had loved Mr Mumford, to the extent that life without him had no longer seemed worth living, went without saying. Of course, this was simply the opinion voiced by women members of the regular crowd. Their menfolk, if trapped in the discussion, either looked sheepish or instantly remembered something pressing that had to be done.

Certain people, Annie Lambert for one, swore she remembered that week in June when Mum had stayed at the hotel with her husband, though for the life of her she couldn't describe what he had looked like, or how tall he was. Nor was she sure of his name. 'Bert', she thought – or perhaps it was 'Stanley'. It was an ordinary sort of name. And she had an inkling that he may have been an insurance agent before he was drafted into the RAF. Not a door-to-door salesman; something a bit grander than that, as one might expect.

'What sort of fellow?' people asked.

'Ordinary,' she said. 'Definitely ordinary.'

'Was he very demonstrative?' Molly Berwick had wanted to know.

'It's a blank,' Annie confessed. 'But I think he called her Rosemary.'

Most people didn't even know her proper name. She had always been Mum to the crowd at the hotel. Not that she was motherly – far from it. True, she was well built, but they all agreed that the twinkle in her coquettish eyes was neither matronly nor maternal. Her friend Mr Armitage, who had cropped up a year or so after her husband went missing, was the perfect partner for her. Not that they were partners except in the companionable sense. Mum certainly wasn't his fancy woman; she wasn't that sort of person, though it was obvious that he thought the world of her. He never addressed her as anything else than Mum, and the others followed suit because Mr Armitage was such a card. They both were. You could bowl people down with a feather, people who weren't in the know, when they heard him calling her Mum, because he looked old enough to be her father. Really, it was comical.

Guests often told the proprietor, Austin White, that he ought to give Mum and Mr Armitage a discount, on account of their entertainment value. In theory, he felt they had a point. They were indeed splendid company, and although a fortnight at the hotel, with full board, was very reasonable, the atmosphere was never quite the same without Mum and Mr Armitage. The things they got up to! The tricks they played! The land-girl had been staying at the hotel for a week now and knew most of the stories by heart. There was the Easter when Mr Armitage painted the horns of all the cows with some sort of luminous paint and then let them loose from their stalls after dark just as Captain Lewis from the Pennines, who'd had a harrowing experience at Arnheim, had come cycling back from the pictures in Welshpool. He was so surprised that he rode his bike into the ditch and cricked his neck. And another time, in the summer probably, Mum had organised a midnight bathing party down at the river and no one had worn costumes, not even the retired bank manager from Norfolk who had some sort of disfigurement and wouldn't have gone naked if Mum hadn't hidden his bathing trunks. That was the marvellous thing about Mum and Mr Armitage – everyone became part of the fun, no one was allowed to stand on the sidelines. To crown it all, there had been a full moon. The stories were endless.

Last night, at supper, someone had complimented Mr White on the floral arrangements, and Albert Ward, one of the regular crowd, had picked up a rose and held it between his teeth. He had caused a riot at the table. Apparently it reminded everybody of the year they had gone with Mum to the flower show at Powys Castle, when Mum had dressed up as a Spanish dancer and persuaded that woman from Manchester, the one with the goitre, to climb ... but the rest of the story had been lost in uproar, and shortly afterwards the regular crowd had left the table and shut themselves up as usual in the library.

'Did you catch what happened the day of the flower show?' the land-girl asked Walter Hood.

'Someone fell,' he said.

'Who?' she asked. But he was looking down at the mourning band on his arm and his eyes were watering.

The next day, shortly before teatime, Miss Emmet was sitting in her mackintosh in the little garden at the side of the hotel, pressing wild flowers between the pages of her nature book, when she was startled to see a procession of guests trooping through the French windows on to the lawn; some of them had obviously just risen from an afternoon nap, because they were still in dressing-gowns and slippers. The man they called Albert Ward was wearing a tea-cosy on his head. From within the hotel came the boom of the dinner gong, struck with frenzy and accompanied by laughter.

'Is it a fire?' asked Miss Emmet, alarmed.

Outside the hotel a dozen people had assembled on the road. Mr and Mrs Hardwick were attempting to keep their children under control, lining them up according to height beneath the library window. One of their daughters, the tomboy child with the plaits, was stabbing a fork into the wistaria which, only yesterday, the proprietor had so carefully and protectively tethered behind a complicated cat's cradle of string. Molly Berwick, the schoolteacher from Huddersfield, and her friend Annie Lambert were standing to attention against the church wall; they had been over at the bowling green and Mrs

Lambert still held the jack. As usual, her friend had a cigarette stuck to her lip.

'Eyes front, girls,' shouted Albert Ward, and he ran into the yard at the back of the hotel and returned with the mucking-out brush, carrying it over his shoulder as though it was a rifle. He began to parade backwards and forwards in front of the porch, barking out military commands like a madman. The diversion this caused gave Mr Hardwick, smiling broadly, the opportunity to snatch the fork from his daughter's hand and smack her quite brutally over the head.

'Whatever is going on?' demanded Miss Emmet, perplexed. She couldn't understand why the child with the plaits wasn't howling.

Then suddenly the two middle-aged men from Wigan – they were always referred to as 'the lads' – who habitually wore shorts, even at supper, and who had been hogging the most comfortable seats in the lounge ever since lunch, snoring, and dangling their speckled legs over the arms of the chintz sofa, rode out of the yard on their tandem bicycle. Wobbling somewhat before gathering speed, they pedalled off down the road towards the hump-backed bridge. The Hardwick children ran in pursuit, whooping like Indians. From the churchyard came a tremendous clatter as rooks lifted from the tops of the elm trees and swooped across the sky.

'Is it a race?' persisted Miss Emmet, not expecting an answer. A few moments later a faint cheer rose from beyond the bridge, and then Mr White's black car, horn tooting like the devil, appeared round the bend of the lane, flanked by the tandem and the screaming children.

'They're here,' shouted Mollie Berwick, stamping her muddy plimsolls up and down on the puddled road. It was hard to believe that she was a teacher.

'They're here,' echoed Annie Lambert, and she sent the

jack hurtling like a cannonball into the hedge.

The regular crowd surged forwards. Without a second's hesitation the land-girl ran behind, clapping her hands.

Miss Emmet went back into the garden. Collecting her nature book from the bench, she let herself out by the wicker gate and set off in the direction of the village. She could hear the telegraph wires humming, high and quivering above her head. Unaccountably, after days of rain the sun came out.

When Miss Emmet returned some hours later, the gong had already sounded for supper. The din from the dining-room could be heard outside on the road. As a general rule she would have gone without food rather than sit down at the table in her walking clothes, but there was a delicious smell of casseroled rabbit above the scent of roses in the garden and her long tramp in the sunshine had increased her appetite. She didn't think she would look out of place in her tweed skirt; the majority of the guests seemed to favour casual attire of one sort or another. On the night of her arrival, when she had come downstairs in one of her two silk frocks, Albert Ward had remarked that they didn't stand on ceremony at the Herbert Arms Hotel. 'So I gather,' Miss Emmet had replied, for she had found herself seated next to the stouter of the two 'lads', and when she bent to pick up her napkin which had fallen to the floor, she inadvertently brushed his hairy leg with her arm. He had made some innuendo, and one or two people had sniggered. She had pretended to be amused.

Miss Emmet went round the front of the hotel into the yard and through the scullery door. Fortunately she had left her court shoes in the cellar when changing into her brogues that morning. The spaniel dog was nosing its tin bowl across the flagstones, ferociously lapping water. Miss Emmet kept her distance. It was not that she was afraid of dogs, simply that she disliked not being able to tell at a glance whether they be friend or foe. It was difficult, she felt, to trust anyone, man or beast, whose eyes gave nothing away. Washing the blackberry stains from her hands at the scullery sink, she went down the passage to change her shoes.

She was just stooping to undo her laces when she realized that she was not alone. There was a man in the cellar, standing on a three-legged stool among the barrels of beer, doing something to the trap door in the ceiling. She was flustered, and stared at him quite rudely.

'Sssh,' the man warned, and he tapped the side of his nose meaningfully with his little finger. Miss Emmet was taken aback. All the same, she found herself going on tiptoe out of the cellar. She was leaning awkwardly against the larder door, one shoe off and one on, when he came after her. 'Joke time,' he whispered. 'It will be our little secret,' And he bounded off down the passage in his striped blazer.

It was difficult for Miss Emmet to get to sleep that night. The noise from the rooms below, the shouting, the gusts of laughter, continued well into the small hours, long after the public bar had closed and the last customer had relieved himself against the cowshed wall beneath her window and gone squelching away up the muddy yard.

As soon as supper had finished, Mr Armitage, assisted by Albert Ward and supervised by Mum, had shoved the long table to the far end of the dining-room before carrying the oval table through from the library.

'What game are we playing?' the regular crowd had wanted to know, bumping into each other and ferrying chairs from one corner to another. Miss Emmet hadn't waited to find out.

Whatever sort of game it was, it was obviously complicated and of long duration. At one point it necessitated the singing of a negro spiritual, at which the spaniel set up a melancholy howling. It woke the collie dog in its kennel. Though Miss

Emmet stuffed her fingers into her ears she still heard the brute's strangled yelps as it hurled itself the length of its chain beyond the pig-sty. Shortly before dawn she thought there was a sound of glass breaking.

Miss Emmet breakfasted alone. Even the children had not yet come down. Mr White hardly spoke when he brought in the fried bacon. None of the windows appeared to be broken.

At midday Miss Emmet bought some buns at the village shop and ate them in a field down by the river. It was annoying to miss a meal already paid for, but she felt she couldn't face luncheon at the hotel.

Last night at supper both Mum and Mr Armitage had addressed her directly. Mr Armitage had asked her what part of the world she came from, and having been told, declared it a lovely spot, which it wasn't by any stretch of the imagination, being not far from the centre of Wolverhampton and dreadfully built up, and Mum, prompted by some absurd remark of Albert Ward's to the effect that Miss Emmet was a child of nature – always messing about with flowers – had promised to send her a box of geranium cuttings. 'And she means it, you know,' cried the schoolteacher. 'It's not one of those comments thrown out at random. Mum always keeps her word.' Miss Emmet had not doubted her. She had already observed how cleverly Mum apportioned each guest his share of the limelight, how unfailingly she hit upon the one topic that suited – and oh, how unstintingly, without ever taking her attention off the speaker or averting the gaze of those light brown eyes ringed with spiky lashes, she passed the salt, the bread, the greens. Really, she had quite ordinary eyes, but for the moment, hunched beside the river, Miss Emmet thought of them as frightening, not for what they had seen, but for what they hadn't.

Later that afternoon, when she was sitting in the garden

waiting for the gong to sound for tea, Miss Emmet overheard the land-girl and Mrs Hardwick discussing the events of the night before. 'It was so unexpected,' Mrs Hardwick was saying. 'I know, I know,' the land-girl said. 'If you ask me, it was uncanny. Uncanny.' And she gave a little scream.

'But such fun,' admitted Mrs Hardwick.

'Not for him,' said the girl and, laughing, they both sat up in their deck chairs and looked guiltily across the garden to where Walter Hood lay on his back in the shade of the hedge.

When they had recovered, Mrs Hardwick called out, 'I expect it wasn't much fun for you either. I don't suppose *you* got much sleep.'

'I always sleep very soundly,' Miss Emmet said. 'Last night was no exception.'

Mrs Hardwick expressed surprise. 'I thought we made enough racket to raise the dead,' she said.

At which the land-girl started to laugh all over again – in the circumstances it was such an apt remark – and then both she and Mrs Hardwick began to recount the story from the beginning, not so much for Miss Emmet's benefit as because neither of them could bear to let the subject drop.

First Mr Armitage had moved the table from the library into the dining-room; in the process a little bit of wallpaper had been scuffed off from under the light switch, but Mum said it was hardly noticeable. Mr Armitage said that if they wanted to get in touch with the spirit world it was always better to choose the oldest part of a house for the setting. Really they should have gone down into the cellar, but Mr Armitage said it was too difficult to transport the table, so the next best thing was to be in the room directly above. He'd done a lot of it in India apparently, when it was too wet to do anything else.

'When it rained,' interrupted the girl, 'even the books turned mouldy.'

'Not mouldy,' objected Mrs Hardwick. 'Just limp.'

They had tried to get in touch with the spirits, but the wine glass kept spelling out 'Shut up' whenever Albert Ward asked if there was anyone waiting on the other side. It was a scream. Of course some people weren't taking it seriously, and Mum said that was probably what was causing the interference.

'He took it seriously,' the land-girl said, lowering her voice and pointing discreetly at the prone figure on the grass.

'Yes,' said Mrs Hardwick, solemn for the moment, and then she was off again.

The glass had finally whizzed straight off the table and hit the window. Mr White had looked a bit put out, but there was no damage. Then Mum told an eerie story of an aunt of hers who had levitated right up to the rafters during a church service. She was in the choir at the time. So they had all stood in a circle round Molly Berwick and put their hands on top of her head, the way Mr Armitage instructed, and pressed down. They sang 'Shall we gather by the river', because Mr Armitage thought it would help, though not all of them were sure of the words. Nothing happened except that Molly complained of feeling dizzy; that, and of the havoc they were causing to her permanent wave.

'Don't forget the dog,' squealed the girl, and for a time Mrs Hardwick almost choked laughing.

Then Mr Armitage said they ought to stand in a line facing the hearth, on account of the mirror above the fireplace. Mirrors, especially oval ones, were known to be conducive to the appearance of phenomena. If they all stood in a line and really concentrated, particularly the doubting Thomases, perhaps there would be some sign. And by Golly, it worked.

'Oh, it did,' shrieked the girl, 'It did. It was uncanny.'

Mr Armitage had missed it all. He'd just that minute popped out to get himself another gin and tonic, and while he was away the carpet rose in the air. Not all in one piece like in the *Thief of Baghdad* but in the middle. They all saw it. Mr Armitage said afterwards that he could kick himself, missing it like that.

'And then *he* got a bit upset,' whispered the land-girl, winking and gesticulating in the direction of Walter Hood 'He was moaning. When the carpet fell flat again he got down on his hands and knees to study it. And then suddenly he shouted and clutched his nose. He hadn't been drinking.'

'Something went up it,' explained Mrs Hardwick 'He said it felt like a bit of wire.'

'He bled,' said the girl.

'Not badly,' protested Mrs Hardwick.

'He called for his mother,' the girl said, and in spite of herself she couldn't stop laughing.

At teatime, and again at supper, Mum apologised to Miss Emmet for the rowdiness of the night before. 'How we must have disturbed you,' she said. 'It was very thoughtless.'

'Please don't mention it,' Miss Emmet had replied on the first occasion, and on the second, 'I may be old, but I hope I'm not a spoil-sport.'

After supper Mum said that she could do with an early night, though it was hard to believe it. She had changed from her matador trousers into a grey costume with square shoulders. In her sling-back shoes, her silk scarf, blood-red, which she wore turban-fashion about her head, she looked ready for a night on the town – had there been one. 'We could all do with an early night,' she insisted, and everyone agreed with her. The land-girl, bitterly disappointed, nodded vehemently.

Miss Emmet was about to go out of the dining-room door when the spaniel padded across the threshold. She stepped aside to let it pass.

'You don't like dogs, do you?' said Mum.

'No, I don't,' Miss Emmet said, and could have bitten off her tongue.

The rest of the week was relatively uneventful. Albert Ward grazed his knees – it had something to do with an egg-and-spoon race organised by Mr Armitage – and one of the Hardwick daughters fell out of an apple tree while watching the bowls tournament. She had been told to stay on the ground. Luckily Mum broke the child's fall, and one of her own fingernails in the process. It was ironic really; the child involved wasn't particularly in favour at the time, having been caught dragging the stuffed stoat on a piece of string along the corridor. The child knew perfectly well that the stoat was anathema to Mum. Everyone did. Fortunately Mum had been out playing tennis. There was also an incident, recounted to Miss Emmet by the land-girl, in which someone had dressed up in a white sheet and flitted about the churchyard, frightening the life out of Mrs Lambert and another guest, who may or may not have had a heart condition, but no harm resulted.

The land-girl had become almost one of the regular crowd, though not all of them remembered her name. She had taken to painting her toenails, and wore turbans, night and day, in imitation of Mum. On the Sunday, as Miss Emmet was coming downstairs ready for church, Mr Armitage called out to her from the bar parlour. He and Mum were without company for once. Reluctantly she went through to them. Mr Armitage asked if he might be allowed to buy her a drink.

'Oh, no,' said Miss Emmet. 'I don't drink, and besides I'm just on my way to church.'

'So are we,' he said. 'There's plenty of time.' And he took her by the elbow and practically forced her to sit down. It wasn't yet opening hours and Mr White was out bell-ringing, but Mr Armitage felt so much at home that he nipped behind the counter and poured out two gin and tonics and a glass of lemonade. 'Drink up,' he said, setting the glass before her. And obediently Miss Emmet sipped at the fizzy liquid, for, although it was a long time ago, she had once been used to doing what men told her.

Neither he nor Mum were dressed for church. He wore his blazer, and Mum was wearing grey flannel trousers and a jacket to match. Her white turban was printed all over with the heads of dogs.

'We were wondering,' said Mum, 'if you'd care to come for a run this afternoon. Just the three of us. Mr White has offered the loan of his car.'

'Do come,' Mr Armitage urged.

'Well, now,' Miss Emmet told them, 'I was thinking of writing letters.'

'It would give us so much pleasure,' said Mum.

Miss Emmet couldn't help smiling; it was such a ridiculous statement.

Mistaking that smile, Mr Armitage cried out jubilantly, 'Jolly good,' and took the matter as settled.

During morning service Miss Emmet prayed that Mum would think of something better to do with her afternoon. She and Mr Armitage had changed their minds about coming to church, and it was not beyond the bounds of possibility that even at this moment they were driving off into the countryside. But when she came out into the sunshine the first thing she saw was the black motor-car parked against the hedge.

She hardly touched her lunch. Not for years had anyone sought her company, and the thought of two hours, one hundred and twenty minutes, in which Mum and Mr Armitage would give her their undivided attention, interrogating her, raking over all the small details of her life, took away her appetite. She considered hiding in her room. But then, how would she deal with the rest of the week?

Mr Armitage gallantly helped her into the back seat of the car. There was a smell of fertiliser and warm leather. Mum sat at the front. The land-girl hovered in the porch of the hotel, hoping to be included even at this late stage. Mum gave her a cheerful wave as they drove off. A Hardwick child ran with them as far as the corner. 'Little pest,' said Mum.

They took the Marton road towards Corndon and the heather-covered slopes of the mountain, winding uphill between fields of barley hedged with hawthorn.

'What a beautiful day,' said Mr Armitage.

'Beautiful,' murmured Mum, dangling her hand outside the window as though the breeze were the sea. Miss Emmet, with her hat on, said nothing.

They reached a plateau of moorland above Marton. Mr Armitage stopped the car and got out to stretch his legs. Mum appeared to be asleep; her turbaned head lolled against the window. Miss Emmet too fell into a doze. Presently Mr Armitage returned and they drove on.

After perhaps half an hour the car stopped again. Waking, Miss Emmet saw that they were at a crossroads. On her right, some few yards down the lane, stood ornamental gates, flanked by posts topped with stone birds, green with moss. The gates were open.

'Oh, look,' said Mum. 'Do let's go in. I love old houses.'

'We'll be trespassing,' said Mr Armitage, and looking over his shoulder asked Miss Emmet what she thought. Miss Emmet said she had no idea.

'Please, said Mum. 'We can say we took a wrong turning.'

They drove up a dark avenue of towering rhododendron, and emerged into the sunlight beside a kitchen garden, beyond which squatted a brick bungalow with vulgar shutters at the windows. An ugly baytree stood in a tub on the brick front step.

'Oh dear,' said Mum. 'How disappointing.'

'They're obviously away,' Mr Armitage said, and he pointed at the runner beans withering on their canes.

'I'd be away if I lived somewhere like that,' remarked Mum, quite fiercely, and Miss Emmet was surprised, for she had imagined Mum as living in just such a house, though without the grounds.

'There's a water tap,' said Mr Armitage. 'And a hose-pipe. Those plants could do with a spot of moisture.' He turned again to Miss Emmet 'What do you think?'

'Don't be silly,' said Mum.

'It does seem a shame,' Miss Emmet said, looking at the shrunken lettuces, the parched blackcurrant bushes, and making up her mind she opened the car door and struggled out.

'Don't blame me if you're caught,' called Mum.

Miss Emmet had advanced some way down the path towards the water tap – Mr Armitage had not yet left the car – when she heard the dog. Its howl was deep-chested, threatening; it was an awful sound. Miss Emmet froze on the path, clutching her old woman's coat about her, too frightened to breathe. Joke time, she thought, knowing she had been caught.

The Alsatian that bounded round the side of the bungalow was jet-black, huge. It was followed by a smaller, emaciated red setter with a mean and bony head. The ferocity of their barking, the slither of their claws on the gravel as they rounded the fence almost drove Miss Emmet out of her mind. Both dogs stopped ten yards from her, ears flat, teeth bared.

Someone screamed, but it was not Miss Emmet. She was concentrating on the red setter; he was the leader, she was sure of it. If she transmitted her fear the brute would go for her throat. She forced herself to look into its hateful eyes. It lay down on the path, snarling.

Miss Emmet heard the click of the car door as it opened behind her. 'Don't move,' she called out, keeping her voice as steady as she could manage. 'You mustn't move.' She could smell mint in the garden, and thyme, and saw dust spiralling upwards in the sunlight as the dog's heart thumped in its chest against the path.

After minutes had elapsed, or it might have been hours, Miss Emmet began to move backwards in the direction of the car. The setter wrinkled its muzzle and half rose. Miss Emmet halted. The dog crouched again.

It took an age. Once, the dog ran forward alarmingly, but this time it stopped of its own accord, and Miss Emmet continued to move backwards, slowly, slowly, and now she had only to put out a hand and she would touch the bonnet of the car.

'Close the windows,' she said, and waited. 'Now, open the door on my side.'

But it was already open for her, and she was through it and scrabbling to slam it shut as the red setter hurled itself against the glass, the Alsatian leaping like a dolphin as high as the roof, slobbering as it snapped its jaws, flecking the windows with spittle.

Mr Armitage said it was an outrage, a disgrace; she might have been mauled to death. The village constable must be told. Only a madman would go on holiday leaving that sort of dog roaming at will. His hands shook on the wheel.

Miss Emmet sensed, rather than saw, the road stretching ahead, the fields beyond, the distant mountain, all permeated by the clear and golden light of the afternoon. There was no shade anywhere, no darkness, except in her heart.

Mum was crying. Twice, she swivelled round on her seat as though she meant to say something to Miss Emmet, but the tears just ran down her cheeks, and she turned away again. Her head in its scarf patterned with dogs wobbled as she wept. But then, thought Miss Emmet, tears were cheap.

The land-girl was disappointed when Mum failed to come down for her usual drink at six o'clock. And during supper she found Mum subdued, not quite up to par. When she attempted to tell her what had happened that afternoon at the bowling green – it was an amusing story and featured one of the 'lads' – Mum cut her short and spoke instead to Miss Emmet, who had caught the sun and whose eyes blazed in her scorched face. Mum talked to no one else during the entire meal. On the few occasions Miss Emmet bothered to reply her tone of voice was peculiarly condescending. Everyone noticed it, or at least the members of the regular crowd, of whom the land-girl was now one.

As soon as the pudding plates had been cleared away, Mum went up to her room. Eyebrows raised, the crowd looked at Mr Armitage. 'She's a little under the weather,' he explained, and left the table.

He went upstairs to her room and did his best to comfort her. He said the ordinary things, the right things; that she mustn't punish herself, that she was not to blame.

'I know,' she said, 'I know.' But oh, how she blamed herself. If she had not insisted on their driving up to that awful house it would never have happened. Miss Emmet was such a frail woman, such a lonely woman. How she must have suffered, not only this afternoon but through all the other afternoons of her solitary life in which she had stood alone, facing fearsome beasts.

'She wouldn't let me go to her,' said Mr Armitage, distressed at the implication. 'I tried, but she told me to keep still. You heard her.'

'I know,' said Mum, and she wept afresh.

It was the land-girl's turn to make the tea and fetch the cheese and biscuits – at this time of the evening Mr White was busy in the bar – but before going through into the kitchen she went upstairs to the first floor. The Hardwick children slept in No.4, and they, of course, were downstairs at the supper table. She was in and out in a jiffy, the stoat in her arms. It would be such a joke.

She had just closed the door of No.1 behind her, the small room at the back overlooking the cowshed, when she heard muffled voices coming from Mum's room. No matter how hard she strained to hear the words she could make neither head nor tail of them, but Mum was upset, that much was obvious. Bursting with curiosity, the land-girl went downstairs to put on the kettle.

'Something's up,' she announced importantly as she carried in the tray, and then stopped; she had forgotten that Miss Emmet was still at the table.

Mr Armitage and Mum appeared again shortly before nine o'clock. As soon as they entered the room Miss Emmet rose from her chair by the fire. It was quite marked, the way she left just as they came in.

Some of the crowd went into the library to play cards. Molly Berwick and Mrs Lambert sat with Mum at the dining-room table. They whispered together, as though there was illness in the house. Mr Armitage sat by the fire, alone, and saw monsters in the flames.

Miss Emmet had felt ill during supper. Undressing in her tiny room, she began to shudder. Such a reaction was only to be expected, she told herself, and pulling back the sheets she climbed into her bed.

At first she thought the thing in her bed was a dead dog,

and that too was to be expected. A moment before she had been feverish; now, cold with anger, she put on her dressing-gown and slippers, and holding the stoat by one leg so that its sawdust blood dripped onto the floorboards, she went in search of Mum.

Talking it over with her friends had done Mum the world of good. Molly Berwick had practically proved that Miss Emmet was almost entirely at fault. No one had asked her to get out of the car, certainly not Mum, who by her own admission had said it was a silly thing to do. And in any case, no harm had come from it, though – God knows – it sounded a close thing. Miss Emmet hadn't been scratched, let alone bitten, and if she had been going to suffer a heart attack from the experience, she would have had one there and then, on the path, or coming home in the car.

'I do feel better,' Mum said 'Thank you.'

'What are friends for?' asked Molly, and only fleetingly did Mum wonder if she knew the answer.

It was at that precise moment that Miss Emmet thrust open the door and ran into the room. She was carrying the stuffed stoat in her arms, and wore her hair net. 'I have known all kinds of people,' said Miss Emmet, 'rich and poor, stupid and intelligent, but none of them have exhibited the degree of malice to be found in you. It is obvious that you have never known what it is to be vulnerable or unhappy.'

It was an impressive speech, and they looked at her with respect, though some had not understood what she said. Mum couldn't make out what it was she held in her arms. At first she thought it was some kind of fur tippet, stiffened with age. Lifting the stoat into the air with both hands, Miss Emmet flung it at her. The stoat skimmed above the table, raking Mum's turban from her head, and bounced on the floor behind the gramophone.

1. Mum and Mr Armitage

Afterwards those of the regular crowd who had been in the bar or in the library said that they were glad to have missed the excitement. They could not have borne the sight of Mum, humiliated at the table, the waxen skin of her burnt scalp shining like an egg in the lamplight. So they said.

2

Beggars Would Ride

On 22 December 1605, two men on horseback, cloaks billowing, hoofs striking sparks from the frozen ground, rode ferociously from the Guildhall to a hill near the village of Hampstead. Dismounting some yards from the summit and a little to the east, they kicked a shallow depression in the earth. Several villagers, knowing in advance the precise and evil properties of the talisman they carried, gawped from a safe distance. Dropping to their knees, the horsemen buried a small round object wrapped in a piece of cloth. Upon rising, the taller of the two men was heard to observe that he wished he was in front of a warm hearth; at which moment the earth erupted and belched fire. For an instant the men stood transfixed and then, cloaks peeled by dancing flame, they whirled upwards, two lumps of burning rag spinning in a blazing arc against the sky.

On the Friday before Christmas, Ben Lewis and Frobisher met as usual in the car park behind the post office. Ben Lewis arrived a quarter of an hour late and, grimacing through the windscreen of his estate car, proceeded to take off his shoes. It annoyed Frobisher, still left waiting in the cold. When the wind stirred the dead leaves on the concrete ground, there was a sound like rats scampering.

'Bloody parky,' shouted Frobisher, but the man in the car was now out of sight, slumped between seat and clutch as he struggled to remove his trousers.

Frobisher, chilled to the bone, jogged to the boundaries of the car park and back again, passing two women seated inside a green Mini, one reading a newspaper, the other noticeably crying.

Ben Lewis emerged wearing shorts and a pair of white sneakers with blue toecaps.

'There's two women back there,' Frobisher told him. 'By the wire netting. One's blubbing into a handkerchief.'

'Really,' said Ben Lewis.

'The other's reading,' said Frobisher. He looked down at Ben Lewis's sneakers and smiled insincerely.

'They're new,' he said. Privately he thought them ridiculous; his own plimsolls, though stained and short on laces, were otherwise all that they should be.

Ben Lewis unlocked the boot of his car and took out a long canvas bag. 'Let's go into the bushes,' he shouted, and ducking through a gap in the fence shouldered his way into a dense undergrowth of alder and old privet.

The ground was liberally strewn with broken glass and beer cans. 'Funny,' remarked Ben Lewis, 'how few whatsits one sees these days.'

'Don't follow you,' said Frobisher.

'Contraceptives,' said Ben Lewis, whose mind was often on such things.

Labouring over the rusted frame of a child's pushchair, Frobisher stubbed his toe on a small, round object half buried beneath decaying leaves. 'I wish,' he panted, 'we could get the hang of the game. Just for an hour or so.'

Twice a week, during the lunch hour, they played tennis together. Frobisher worked just across the road in the

National Westminster Bank, and Ben Lewis drove from Hampstead where he was a partner in a firm of estate agents.

'Whose turn is it to pay?' asked Frobisher, when, out of breath, they reached the entrance to the tennis courts.

He always asked that. He knew perfectly well that he had paid on Wednesday. He had a horror of being thought mean.

'Yours,' said Ben Lewis, who had no such fears.

The attendant marked them down for Court 14, which was listing slowly and surrounded on three sides by trees. Though the court itself was full of pot-holes and the net invariably wound too high, it did have the advantage of privacy. Neither Frobisher nor Ben Lewis cared to be watched. When they had first started to play together, having chummed up in a pub in Belsize Park and mutually complained of being unfit, they had imagined it would be a matter of weeks before their game improved. Both had last played, slackly, at school. A year had passed and improvement had not come. Ben Lewis's service was quite good but he gained little advantage from it because it was too good for Frobisher to return. Frobisher had a nice forehand of a sort, the sort that lobbed the ball high into the air. Ben Lewis couldn't see the ball unless it came low over the net. They comforted themselves with the thought of the benefit they obviously derived from bending down and trotting about in the open air.

Of the two, Ben Lewis was the more outwardly narcissistic. He used aftershave and he hinted that he'd once had a sauna. He worried about his hair, which was now sparse, and the way his cheeks were falling in. He felt it was all right for Frobisher to sport a weathered crown – his particular height and porky-boy belly put him into a defined category – but he himself was on the short side and slender. He didn't want to degenerate into an elderly whippet with emaciated flanks, running like hell after the rabbit in the Waterloo Cup, and balding into the bargain.

'People are awfully callous these days, aren't they?' said Frobisher.

'What?' said Ben Lewis.

'The way they read while other people cry.'

'I shouldn't care for it,' said Ben Lewis. 'Not outdoors. Not in this weather.' He pushed open the rusted gate to Court 14 and began to unzip his bag.

'How's Margaret?' asked Frobisher.

'Fine, fine,' said Ben Lewis. He didn't inquire after Frobisher's wife. Not any more. Frobisher's wife was called Beth, and Ben Lewis, who some years ago had directed *Little Women* for his local Amateur Dramatic Society, had once referred to her jokingly of course, as 'Keep Death Off the Road'. Frobisher, not having seen the play, hadn't seen the joke. Far from it. He'd made some pretty silly remarks about it sounding disrespectful to his wife. Ben Lewis thought it was hypocritical of him, seeing that Frobisher had admitted to having a woman on the side. The previous summer, when excessive heat had forced Frobisher to remove his shirt, he had positively boasted about the two scratch marks Ben Lewis had noticed on his back. At the time, Ben Lewis had thought of rubbing his own back against a rose bush in his front garden, only he forgot.

Frobisher removed his overcoat and scarf and was discovered to be wearing a dark-blue tracksuit with white stripes on each shoulder.

'That's new,' said Ben Lewis, smiling insincerely. He had the strangest notion, when he strolled into position on the court, that his new shoes had springs in the heel.

Without warning, Frobisher hit a very good ball down the line. Ben Lewis returned it, though he was dazzled as usual by the horizontal of the grimy net and the glittering rectangles of the tower block built lower down the hill. For perhaps half a remarkable minute they successfully kept the ball in play until Ben Lewis, misjudging his own strength, sent it flying into the wire netting with such force that it lodged there like some unlikely fruit. 'You won't believe it,' he told Frobisher. 'But I thought the net was higher or you were lower.'

'Optical illusion,' said Frobisher kindly, scrambling up the grass bank to pluck the ball from the wire. 'It's that jetstream.' And he indicated with his racket two white and wobbling lines stretched across the sky. He felt unusually light on his feet and remarked confidently that it was all a question of rhythm. He could feel, he asserted, a definite sense of rhythm creeping into his stroke. They were both exhilarated at this sudden improvement in form. Secretly, Ben Lewis thought it had something to do with his shoes. Frobisher openly expressed the belief that his tracksuit had contributed to his new-found skill.

'A fellow in the office,' said Ben Lewis, 'started to get into trendy trousers last summer. His wife egged him on. He pulled off a fairly complicated land deal in South Woodford.'

'Direct result, you mean?' said Frobisher.

'Nothing was ever proved,' replied Ben Lewis, and he bounced on his toes and served with quite extraordinary speed and verve.

After a quarter of an hour an awed Ben Lewis said that in his opinion they were Wimbledon standard and possibly better than that bad-tempered fellow on the box who was always arguing with the man up the ladder. 'And you're right about the rhythm,' he said. He kept to himself the fanciful idea that they were dancing a slow fox-trot, championship standard, not a foot wrong, every move correctly timed, sweeping backwards and forwards across the court to the beat of an invisible orchestra.

Frobisher would have given anything for his wife Beth to have been watching him. She was always telling the children that he had no sense of co-ordination. It struck him as absurd that only last week he and Ben Lewis, trailing towards the bushes to return to the car park, had openly sneered at the dedicated players on Court 12. The tall man with the sweat-band round his head, who was generally there on Wednesday and Friday, had caused them particular amusement – 'that ass with the hair ribbon', as Ben had called him. Frobisher wondered if it would be going too far to have a band round his own forehead.

It came to Ben Lewis, fleetingly, sadly, as he arched his back in preparation for a particularly deadly service, how different things might have been if he had always played like this. Only once in his life had he experienced applause, at the curtain call of *Little Women* in East Finchley. In imagination he multiplied the volume of that first, last and giddy applause, and flinging his racket to the linesman leaped, gazelle-like, over the net.

After a further twenty inspired minutes, Frobisher suggested that perhaps they should rest. Though perspiring, neither of them was the least tired.

'I do feel,' said Ben Lewis, with a touch of hysteria, 'that we might be hospital cases tomorrow.' Weak with laughter they flopped down on the sodden bench at the side of the court and lolled against each other.

'Doing anything for Christmas?' asked Frobisher at last. It was better to behave as if everything was normal.

'Usual thing,' said Ben Lewis. 'Margaret's mother, Margaret's mother's sister ... that sort of thing. What about you?'

'Nothing special,' said Frobisher. 'Just me and Death.' From beyond the trees came the fragmented screams of children running in the playground of the Catholic school.

'Do you think,' said Frobisher, unable to contain himself,

'that it's the same thing as riding a bike?'

'A knack, you mean,' said Ben Lewis. 'Once learnt, never lost?'

'Yes,' said Frobisher.

'Maybe,' said Ben Lewis. But he didn't think it was. They both fell silent, reliving the last three-quarters of an hour, until Frobisher remarked generously that Ben Lewis might have won the last set if the ground hadn't been so full of pot-holes. 'Not your fault,' he added. 'It was jolly bad luck.'

Ben Lewis found that he was gripping the edge of the bench so tightly that a splinter of wood pierced his finger. He knew that if he relaxed his hold he would spring upward and in one bound rip from the rusted fence a length of wire to tie round Frobisher's neck. He said as calmly as he was able, 'I don't believe in luck, bad or otherwise.'

From the playground came the blast of a whistle. The chattering voices receded as the children flocked indoors. Frobisher stood up, and, adjusting the top half of his tracksuit, strode purposefully back to his previous position on the court. 'My service,' he called curtly.

His first ball bounced low on the ground. Ben Lewis, gripping his racket in both hands as if running in an egg-and-spoon race, stumbled forward and scooped it skywards. It flew over his head, over the wire, and vanished into the trees.

'My God,' said Frobisher. He stood with one hand on his hip and gazed irritably at Ben Lewis. 'You'd better retrieve it,' he ordered, as though Ben Lewis were a dog. He watched his opponent lumber through the gate and heard him squelch down the muddy path in the direction of the attendant's hut. Frobisher took a running jump at the net and hurdled it with ease.

Ben Lewis, passing Court 12, saw that the man with the

sweat-band round his head had a new opponent. A woman. She was crouching down, racket held in both hands, head swinging from side to side like a bull about to charge.

Having skirted the attendant's hut and entered the bushes, Ben Lewis tried to visualise the flight path of the erratic ball. He was probably not far enough back. He tried to clamber up the the bank to see if Court 14 was visible, but the bushes grew too thickly. He scuffed with his shoes at the broken glass and refuse, thinking his search was hopeless, and almost at once uncovered the missing ball. He bent down and picked it up. He was now sweating and the muscles in his legs were trembling. He found he held not only the ball but something round and small clinging to a scrap of rotting cloth. Shivering with revulsion, he flung both ball and rag away from him and wiped his hands on his shorts.

He wished he was in a nice hot bath ...

Frobisher, fretting on Court 14, was startled by the noise of steam escaping from some large funnel. He supposed it came from the ventilation system of the tower block further down the hill. When he looked in the direction of the car park he observed a large white cloud drifting above the trees. He went in pursuit of his opponent. Struggling through the bushes calling Ben Lewis's name, he was astonished to see that the ground had been swept clear of rubbish. Ben Lewis's car was still parked near the fence. The woman at the steering-wheel of the green Mini said she hadn't seen anybody, she'd been too busy reading.

'Didn't you hear that noise?' asked Frobisher severely. 'Like a train stopping. A puffer train.'

The woman stared at him. 'Perhaps he's just gone home,' she suggested.

'He's not wearing trousers,' said Frobisher. He retraced his steps to Court 14 and found it deserted.

Frobisher told his colleagues in the bank that his friend Ben Lewis had in some mysterious way disappeared. They weren't interested. Most of them thought Frobisher a bit of a slouch.

Before it grew dark, Frobisher slipped over the road to see if Ben Lewis's car was still near the gap in the fence. It was. Frobisher went into the bushes again and this time found the tennis ball and a smooth round object lying side by side on the ground.

He wished he knew where Ben Lewis had gone ...

3

The Longstop

Words and cricket seem to go together. Whenever I watch the game, by mistake, on television, I think it's not true that you can't get blood from a stone.

I only ever played the game once myself, in the park with some evacuees from Bootle. I was allowed to join in because I held a biscuit tin filled with shortbread that my mother had baked. They said I could have a turn if I gave them a biscuit afterwards. I didn't make any runs because I never hit the ball, and when I kept my promise and began to open the tin the evacuees knocked me over and took every piece of shortbread. They threw the tin over the wall into the gentlemen's lavatory. I had to tell my mother a six-foot-high naughty man with a Hitler moustache had chased me; she would have slapped me for playing with evacuees.

Mr Baines, who was my maternal grandfather, was a lover of cricket. Mr Jones, my father, didn't care for the game. He cared even less for my grandfather. In his humble estimation Mr Baines was a mean old bugger, a fifth columnist, and, following his self-confessed denouncing of a neighbour in Norris Green for failing to draw his curtains against the black-out, a Gauleiter into the bargain. He was also a lounge lizard, a term never satisfactorily explained, though it was true that my grandfather fell asleep between meals.

Apart from words, my father was keen on sailing ships. He subscribed to a monthly magazine on the subject. If he was to be believed, he had, when no more than a child, sailed as a cabin boy to America. In middle age, his occupation a commercial traveller, he prowled the deserted shore beyond the railway line, peering of an evening through the barbed wire entanglements at the oil tankers and the black destroyers that crawled along the bleak edge of the Irish Sea; it was a gloomy mystery to him where that fearless lad before the mast had gone.

Every week Mr Baines came for Sunday dinner. There had been a moment at the outbreak of the war when he had contemplated coming to live with us, but after three days he returned home. He said he preferred to take his chances with the Luftwaffe. His conversation during the meal was always about cricket, and mostly to do with a man called Briggs. Briggs, he said, had just missed greatness by a lack of seriousness. If only Briggs had taken batting more seriously he would have been, make no bones about it, the best all-round cricketer in England since W. G. Grace. Briggs, he informed us, took bowling and fielding in deadly earnest, but as a batsman he was a disaster; he seemed far more anxious to amuse the crowd than to improve his average.

Nobody listened to my grandfather, certainly not my father who was often heard to remark quite loudly that, had he been in control, he wouldn't give the old skinflint the time of day, let alone Sunday dinner, world without end.

However, one particular Sunday in the summer of 1944, Mr Baines, without warning, excelled himself when describing a cricketer called Ranjitsinhji.

'Just to set eyes on him,' said Mr Baines, 'was a picture in motion. The way his shirt ballooned –'

'A black chappie,' my father exclaimed, taken aback at my grandfather speaking civilly of a foreigner.

'An Indian Prince,' said Mr Baines. He was equally taken aback at being addressed in the middle of his monologue. He was used to conversing uninterrupted throughout the devouring of the black-market roast pork.

'They're two a penny,' my father said.

'More potatoes?' asked my mother, worriedly.

'Even when it wasn't windy,' continued Mr Baines, 'his shirt ballooned. Whether half a gale was blowing on the Hove ground or there wasn't enough breeze to shift the flag at Lord's, the fellow's shirt flapped like the mainsail of a six-tonner on the Solent.'

'Blithering rubbish,' said my father. He stabbed at a sprout on his plate as though it was alive.

My mother told Mr Baines that they played cricket in the park every Sunday afternoon. Not a proper team, just old men and young lads. Not what he was used to, of course. 'But,' she said, eyeing my father contemptuously, 'it will do us good to get out into the pure air.'

She didn't mean my father to come. We were never a family who went anywhere together. My father's opinion, had he voiced it, would have been that the family who stood together fell out together. Often we would attempt an outing, but between the closing of the back door and the opening of the front gate, misunderstandings occurred and plans were abruptly abandoned. She was astonished when, having washed up and taken off her pinny, she found my father in the hall putting on his trilby hat. She didn't like it, you could tell. Her mouth went all funny and the lipstick ran down at one corner. Shoulder to shoulder, more or less, we set off for the park.

I wanted to nip over the garden fence and through the blackberry bushes into Brows Lane, but my mother said my grandfather wasn't about to nip anywhere, not at his age. We trotted him down the road past the roundabout and the Council offices. The brass band was practising in the hut behind the fire station. When he heard the music, Mr Baines began to walk with his arms held stiffly at his sides, only the band kept stopping and starting and the tune came in bits, and after a little while he gave up playing at soldiers and shuffled instead. My father looked at the ground all the time; there was a grey splodge on the brim of his hat where a pigeon had done its business.

The park was quite grand, even though it had lost its ornamental gates at the entrance. My mother said they'd been removed to make into tanks. My father swore they were mouldering away in a brick field down by the Docks, along with his mother's copper kettle and a hundred thousand front railings. The park had a pavilion, a sort of hunting lodge with mullioned windows and a thatched roof. People were worried about incendiary bombs. The park keeper kept his grass roller inside and buckets of water. In front of the pavilion was a sunken bowling green, and beyond that a miniature clock-golf course. We used to ride our bikes up and down the bumps. Behind the pavilion, within a roped enclosure, was a German Messerschmitt. It had been there for two years. It hadn't crash-landed anywhere near our village; it was on loan. The park keeper was always telling the Council to tell someone to come back for it. At first we had all run round it and shuddered, but after a few weeks we hardly noticed it any more. It just perched there, propped on blocks, one wing tipped up to the sky, the cockpit half burned away, its melted hood glittering beetle-black in the sunlight.

When he saw the aeroplane, my father cried out, 'Good

Lord, look at that!' He flung his arms out theatrically and demanded, 'Why wasn't I told?'

No one took any notice of him; he was always showing off. He stared up at the plane with an expression both fearful and excited, as though the monster was still flying through the air and he might yet be machine-gunned where he stood.

My mother and Mr Baines sat on wooden chairs pressed against the privet hedge. My mother was worried in case we were too near the wicket. She was for ever ducking and flinching, mistaking the white clouds that bowled across the sky for an oncoming ball. It wasn't an exciting game as far as I could tell but my grandfather sat on the edge of his chair and didn't fall asleep once. There was a man fielding who was almost as old as Mr Baines, and when the bowler was rubbing the ball up and down the front of his trousers preparing to run, the old man rested in a deck-chair on the pitch. The butcher's boy from the village shop was crouching down behind the wicket wearing a tin hat and smoking a cigarette.

'That fellow,' said Mr Baines, pointing at the elderly batsman in Home Guard uniform, 'is taking a risk. If he misses the ball he'll be out leg before or he'll get his skull stove in.'

'Heavens,' cried my mother, cringing backwards on her chair.

'Briggs used to play that sort of stroke,' said Mr Baines. 'Of course, he knew what he was doing.'

My father came and sat down beside him. He said: 'I never knew it was there. I never knew.' He still looked excited. He'd taken his hat off and there was a mark all round his forehead.

'As soon as he saw what ball it was,' Mr Baines said, 'he'd stand straight in front of the wicket and wait until it looked as if it would go straight through his body –'

'I never knew,' repeated my father. 'I never even guessed.'

He was very unobservant. He'd been morosely loping to and from the railway station night and morning for twenty years and never bothered to look through the trees.

'Be quiet,' said my mother. 'We're concentrating.'

'At the last moment,' Mr Baines said, 'Briggs would hook it. Glorious stroke. Poetry in motion.'

'If I could have served,' remarked my father, 'I would have chosen the Merchant Navy.'

'Mind you,' Mr Baines said. 'It had to be a fast ball.'

'Failing that, I think I'd have fancied the Air Force,' said my father.

There wasn't anything one could reply to that piece of poppy-cock. If my father had been healthy enough to join up, he wouldn't have been any use. When Wilfred Pickles said on the wireless, 'And how old are you, luv? Ninety-seven!', my father had to blow his nose from emotion. If he happened to hear 'When the lights go on again all over the world' on Forces' Favourites, he had to go out into the scullery to take a grip on himself. According to my mother, Auntie Doris had turned him into a cissy. He was a terrible cry-baby. He cried one time when the cat went missing. My mother said that most of the time his carrying on like that was misplaced. Once he went all over Southport pressing shilling pieces into the hands of what he called 'our gallant boys in blue'. The were soldiers from the new hospital down by the Promenade. My father told them he was proud of them, that they were the walking wounded; he had a field day with his handkerchief. Afterwards it turned out there was nothing wrong with them, nothing wounded that is, it wasn't that sort of hospital. They were soldiers all right, my mother said, but they'd all caught a nasty disease from just being in the army, not from fighting or anything gallant like that, and it was certainly nothing to be proud of.

'I'm not criticising,' said Mr Baines, looking at the fielder resting in his deck-chair, 'but these fellows lack self-discipline. The true sportsman is a trained athlete. He dedicates himself to the game. Only way to succeed. Same with anything in all walks of life – cotton, fishing, banking, shipping –'

'Doesn't he ever get tired of his own voice?' said my father savagely.

I sat on the grass with my back propped against my mother's knees. I could feel her trembling from indignation. My grandfather began to clap, slapping the palms of his hands together above my head as the elderly batsman left the crease and began to trail towards the pavilion. Mr Baines was the only one applauding; there were few spectators and most of those had swivelled round the other way to look at the bowling green. The new batsman was younger and he had a gammy leg. When he heard Mr Baines clapping he glared at him, thinking he was being made fun of.

'One time,' said Mr Baines, 'Briggs got stale. The Lancashire committee suggested that he should take a week's holiday. He went to a remote village in Wiltshire –'

'Don't think I don't know what the old beggar's getting at,' said my father. 'Talking about cotton like that. Did he think I wanted to come a cropper in cotton –'

'Word got round as it will,' Mr Baines said. 'Second day there a fellow came up to Briggs and asked him how much he'd take for playing in a local match. Ten pound, said Briggs, thinking that would be prohibitive –'

The park was shimmering in sunshine. You couldn't see the boundary by the poplar trees; all the leaves were reflecting like bits of glass. The man with the gammy leg was out almost at once. I didn't know why, the bails were still standing. I couldn't follow the rules. A fat man came out in a little peaked cap. I could hear the dull clop of the ball against the bat and the click of the bowls on the green as they knocked against each other. Behind me the voices went on and on, another game in progress, more dangerous than either cricket or bowls, and the rules were always changing.

'Briggs's side lost the toss,' said Mr Baines, 'and he had to begin the bowling. His first ball was hit out of the ground for six –'

'If I'd had any appreciation all these years,' my father said, 'things might have been different. When I think how I tramp from door to door in all weathers while you and your blasted Dad put your feet up –'

'Finally he had two wickets for a hundred and fifty runs. The crowd was looking quite nasty,' Mr Baines said. 'But what finished them off was that when he went into bat he was bowled second ball.'

'All I needed was a few bob at the right moment,' said my father. 'Just a few measley quid and the old skinflint wouldn't put his hand in his pocket –'

'Don't speak about him like that,' cried my mother. 'I won't have him called names.'

'Only a stalwart policeman and the train to London saved him from a jolly good hiding,' said Mr Baines. 'He never tried village cricket again.'

'If you'd been any proper sort of woman,' groaned my father, 'you'd have been a help-mate.'

'Be quiet,' my mother cried. 'Shut your mouth.'

'You've only been a bloody hindrance,' my father shouted. He jumped up and knocked over his chair. He walked away in the direction of the aeroplane, leaving his hat on the grass.

'What's up?' I asked. Though I knew. 'Is he off home, then?'

'Ssh,' said my mother. 'He's gone for a widdle.' Her voice was all choked.

'Don't upset yourself,' said Mr Baines. 'It's not worth it.'

'He sickens me,' my mother said. 'Sickens me. Whimpering

over the least thing when inside he's like a piece of rock. He's hard. He's got no pity for man nor beast.'

'Don't waste your tears,' said Mr Baines. 'You can't get blood from a stone.'

At that moment the ball flew past the wicket and striking the ground rolled to my grandfather's feet. He leapt up and striding to the side of the pitch chucked the ball at the batsman. He didn't exactly bowl it; he sort of dipped one shoulder and flung the ball like a boy skimming a stone on water. The batsman, taken by surprise at such an accurate throw, swung his bat. The scarlet ball shot over Mr Baines's shoulder and went like a bullet from a gun after my father.

When we ran up to him he was stood there in the shadow of the Messerschmitt with his hand clutched to the side of his head. The ball hadn't hit him full on, merely grazed the side of his temple. But he was bleeding like a pig.

'That's a turn-up for the book,' said Mr Baines.

4
People for Lunch

'We simply must,' said Margaret.

'Do we have to?' asked Richard.

'No,' said Margaret, 'but we will. We've been to them eight weekends on the trot. It looks awful.'

Thinking about it, Richard supposed she was right. Every Sunday throughout May and June they had motored down to Tunbridge Wells, arriving in time for lunch. They had left again at six o'clock, after Dora and Charles had made them a cup of Earl Grey tea. Apart from an obligatory inspection of the kiddies' new bicycles or skate-boards, or being forced to listen to some long feeble jokes told by young Sarah, the hours spent in Dora's well-appointed house had been pleasant and restful. 'I don't think they expect to be asked back,' said Richard. 'They're not like that.'

'Not *expect*,' agreed Margaret. 'But I think we should.'

Dora and Charles were asked for the following Sunday. Richard and Charles had gone to university together, been articled together, and now worked for the same firm of lawyers, in the litigation department. 'Jolly nice of you,' said Charles, when he heard. 'We're looking forward to it.'

It had been a little tricky suggesting to Dora that she leave the children behind. 'They'll be so bored here,' explained Margaret, when speaking to her on the phone. 'As you know we've only a backyard. There's no sun after eleven o'clock in the morning. And Malcolm won't be here.' She didn't feel too awkward about it because after all Dora had a marvellous woman who lived in, and Dora herself was frightfully keen once the penny had dropped.

'How did you put it?' asked Richard worriedly. 'I hope you didn't imply we ...'

'Don't be silly,' said Margaret crossly. 'You know me. I was the soul of tact.'

Two unfortunate events occurred on the morning of the luncheon party. The sky, which earlier had been clear and blue, filled with clouds, and Malcolm, who had promised faithfully he was going out, changed his mind. He said there was a programme he wanted to watch on TV at one o'clock.

'You can't,' wailed Margaret. 'We'll be sitting down for lunch.'

'I'm watching,' said Malcolm. He switched on the set and lay full-length on the wicker couch from Thailand, flicking cigarette ash on to the pine floor.

'Can't watch the telly, old chap,' said Richard bravely. ' 'Fraid not. We've people coming.'

'Piss off,' said Malcolm.

At midday Richard suggested Malcolm come with him to the pub to buy the beer. 'I'm not shifting,' said Malcolm. 'I don't want to miss my programme.'

While Richard was away, the clouds lifted and the sun shone. Margaret looked out of the window at the square of paving stones set with shrubs and bordered by a neat privet hedge. Although only seventeen, Malcolm was extremely tenacious of purpose. He would spend the entire lunch hour jumping up and switching on the telly after Richard had turned it off. The only slight chance of stopping him lay in hitting him over the head, and then there'd be a punch-up and it would undoubtedly spoil the atmosphere. She began to carry chairs through to the front door; if it were not for the privet hedge, they would be sitting practically on the pavement, but it couldn't be helped.

'What the hell are you doing?' asked Richard, when he returned with the drink.

'It's your fault,' cried Margaret shrilly. 'You shouldn't have boxed the television in. I'm not entertaining guests with the damn thing blazing away.' After several harsh words Richard strode into the house and began to manhandle the table into the hall.

'I will not ask you to help,' he called to Malcolm. 'I will not point out that your unreasonable behaviour is the cause of all this upheaval.' He swore as the table, wedged in the narrow passage, crushed his fingers against the jamb of the door.

'Stop muttering,' shouted Malcolm. 'If you've got anything to say, say it to my face.'

The table, once settled on flagstones, sloped only partially at one end. Covered with a tablecloth, a vase of roses placed in the centre, the effect was charming. 'I think it's better than indoors,' said Margaret. 'I really do.'

'I could have a heart attack,' said Richard. ' – We both could – and that boy would trample over us to change channels.'

'Sssh!' said Margaret. 'Don't upset yourself.'

Dora and Charles arrived promptly at twelve-thirty. The moment they stepped out of the car the sun went behind a cloud.

'It's a little informal,' called Margaret gaily, 'but we thought you'd prefer to sit outside.'

'Rather,' said Charles, gazing at the row of bins behind the upright chairs. Richard kissed Dora and Margaret kissed Charles; the merest brush of lips against stubble and powder. 'I'm afraid I haven't shaved,' said Richard.

'Good God,' cried Charles, who had performed this ritual at seven-thirty. 'Who the hell shaves on Sunday?'

They went into the front room and had a drop of sherry, standing in a group at the window and eyeing the table outside as if it were a new car that had just been delivered.

'Lovely roses,' said Charles.

'Home-grown?' asked Dora. They had to shout to be heard above the noise of the television.

'No,' said Margaret. 'We do have roses in the backyard, but the slightest hint of wind and they fall apart.'

'I know the feeling,' said Dora, who could be very dry on occasion.

They all laughed, particularly Dora.

'Belt up,' said Malcolm.

They trooped in and out, carrying the salad bowl and the condiments, the glasses for the wine.

'This is fun,' said Charles, stumbling over a geranium pot and kicking a milk bottle down the steps. He insisted on fetching the dustpan and brush. Malcolm was eating an orange and spitting pips at the skirting board.

'You're doing 'O' levels, I suppose,' said Charles. 'Or is it 'A's?'

'You what?' said Malcolm.

'Any idea what you want to do?' asked Charles, leaning on the handle of the brush.

'Nope,' said Malcolm.

'Plenty of time,' said Charles. He went outside and confided to Richard. 'Nice boy you've got there. Quiet but deep.'

'Possibly,' said Richard uneasily.

It was an enjoyable lunch. Margaret was a good cook and Richard refilled the glasses even before they were empty. It was quite secluded behind the hedge, until closing time. Then a stream of satisfied customers from the pub round the corner began to straggle past the house.

'What's so good about this area of London,' said Richard, after hastily dispatching a caught-short Irishman who had lurched through the privet unbuttoning his flies, 'is that it's not sickeningly middle-class.'

'Absolutely,' agreed Charles, listening to the splattering of water on the pavement behind his chair.

Margaret was lacking spoons for the pudding. 'Please, Charles,' she appealed, touching him briefly on the shoulder.

He ran inside the house glad to be of service. He looked in the drawers and on the draining board.

After a moment Margaret too came indoors. There was no sign of Malcolm. 'Have you found them?' she shouted.

'Stop it,' said Charles.

'They're right in front of your eyes,' she bellowed.

'For God's sake,' he whispered. 'They'll see us.'

He backed away down the room. It was infuriating, he thought, the knack women had of behaving wantonly at the wrong moments. Had they been alone in some private place, depend upon it, Margaret would have been full of excuses and evasions. In all the twelve years he had known her, there had never been a private place. He had wanted there to be, but he hadn't liked to plan it. God knows, life was sordid enough as it was. He didn't know how old Richard stood it – his wife giving off signals the way she did. The amount of lipstick Margaret wore, the tints in her hair, the way everything wobbled when she moved. Dora was utterly different. You could tell just by looking at her that she wasn't continually thinking about men.

'Where's Malcolm?' asked Margaret.

'I've no idea,' he said. He found he was being manoeuvred between a wall cupboard and the cooker. He had never known her so determined. He glanced desperately at the window. All he could see was the back of his wife's head. 'All right, you little bitch,' he said hoarsely. The word excited him dreadfully. It was so offensive. He never called Dora a bitch, not unless they were arguing. 'You've asked for it,' he said. Eyes closed and breathing heavily, he held out his arms. Margaret, looking over her shoulder, was in time to see Richard rising from his chair. He waved. She fled soundlessly from the room.

Dora quite enjoyed being in the front yard. It was handy being so near the dustbins. When the weather was good they often lunched on the lawn in Tunbridge Wells, but there the grass was like a carpet to Charles and he grew livid if so much as a crumb fell to the ground.

'Where's Malcolm gone?' asked Margaret. Richard told her he was in the basement, probably listening to records. Actually he had seen Malcolm sloping off down the street a quarter of an hour before, but he didn't want to worry her. Lately, Malcolm had taken to going out for hours at a stretch and coming home in an elated condition. They both knew it was due to pot-smoking, or worse. In a sense it was a relief to them that he had at last found something which interested him.

'Do you know,' said Charles. 'I do wonder if we're doing the right thing, burying the children down in the country.'

'Oh, come on,' scoffed Margaret. 'All that space and fresh air ... not to mention their ponies.'

'I know exactly what he means,' said Dora. 'They're very protected. When I think of Malcolm at Sarah's age, he was streets ahead of her.'

'Was he?' said Richard.

'Well, he was so assured,' Dora explained. 'Handing round the wine, joining in the conversation. I always remember that time we came for dinner with Bernard and Elsa, and Malcolm hid under the table.'

'I remember that,' said Charles thoughtfully. 'He crapped.' There was a moment's startled silence. 'It was your word,' Charles said hastily, looking at Richard. 'I remember clearly. I said to you, I think Malcolm's had a little accident, and you said to me, Oh dear, he's done a crap. I thought it was marvellous of you. I really did.'

'Really he did,' said Dora.

'I wonder what happened to Elsa,' said Margaret. When they had finished their coffee, Richard fetched a tray and began to gather the dishes together. It had grown chilly.

'Leave those,' said Margaret, shivering.

Dora put on her old cardigan. It hung shapelessly from her neck to her thigh. Peering through the hedge she caught sight of the camellia in next door's garden. 'Isn't it a beauty,' she enthused, waving her woolly arms in excitement.

'I'll show it to you,' offered Richard. 'They won't mind you taking a dekko. They're a nice couple. He's something of a character. He wears Osh-Coshes.'

'Charles,' said Dora. 'Please ring Mrs Antrim. Just to check if the kiddies are all right.'

Obediently Charles went into the house. He was followed by Margaret.

The telephone was on a shelf outside the bathroom door. He couldn't remember the code number. 'Doesn't he remember his little codey-wodey number?' said Margaret, who had been drinking quite heavily.

'Be careful,' he protested. 'The front door's open.'

'They've gone next door to look at the flowers,' she said.

'They might pop back at any moment.'

'Well, come in here then.' And with brute force she pushed him from the phone towards the bathroom.

It was quite flattering in a way, the urgent manner in which she propelled him through the door. He wished her teeth would stop chattering; she was making the devil of a noise. Feeling a bit of an ass, he sat on the edge of the bath while she stood over him and rumpled his hair.

'Steady on,' he said. 'I haven't a comb on me.'

'Kiss me,' she urged. 'Kiss me.'

'Look here,' he said, wrenching her fingers out of his ears. 'This is neither the time nor the place. I can't relax in this kind of situation.'

'Oh, shut up,' she said, and shoved him quite viciously so that he lost his balance and lay half in and half out of the bath. At that instant she thought she heard someone coming up the hall.

'Christ,' she moaned, dropping to one knee and peering through the keyhole. There was no one there. 'Listen,' she told Charles, who was struggling to get out of the bath. 'If they come back, I'll go and you stay here. You can come out later.'

'What if Richard wants to use the lavatory?' he asked worriedly. Margaret said if that happened, he must nip down the steps into the yard and hide in the basement until the coast was clear.

'But what about Malcolm?' asked Charles. 'Malcolm's down there.' Margaret assured him Malcolm would be in the front room of the basement. Even if he did see Charles it wouldn't make much difference – Malcolm hardly said one articulate word from one week to the next.

'If you're sure,' breathed Charles. Half-heartedly he embraced her. He didn't quite know how far he should go. He felt a bit out of his depth. 'Are we ... is it ... should we?' he murmured.

'Play it by ear,' Margaret said mysteriously.

Charles was just unbuttoning his blazer when they both heard footsteps outside. In a flash Margaret was through the bathroom door and closing it behind her. He heard her calling. 'Cooee, I'm here.' Panic-stricken, he undid the bolt of the back door and crept on to the small veranda. Beneath him lay the yard, overgrown with weeds and littered with rose petals. A rambler, diseased and moulting, clung ferociously to the brick wall. Trembling, he descended the steps and inched his way towards the basement door. He stepped into Richard's study, gloomy as the black hole of Calcutta and bare of furniture save for a desk and a chair. Margaret had been right. Malcolm was in the front room playing records. Charles recognised some of the tunes from *Chorus Line*. He wasn't over-fond of modern music but he couldn't help being impressed by the kind of enjoyment Malcolm seemed to be experiencing. There were distinct sighs and moans coming from beyond the wall. He eased himself into Richard's chair and waited for Margaret to send some sort of signal. The amount of paperwork Richard brought home was staggering. No wonder poor old Margaret behaved badly. Of course she didn't have any hobbies or attend evening classes. She wasn't like Dora, who was out several nights a week at French circles and history groups. He supposed things were different in the country. For some reason he felt terribly sleepy – probably nerves at being in such an absurd situation. He began to shake with weak and silent laughter and, when it was over, fell into a peaceful doze.

He was awakened by a shower of spoons clattering on to the flagstones outside the window. The record in the next room had been turned off. Cautiously he advanced into the yard and peered upwards. Someone was standing at the kitchen window. Adopting what he hoped was a casual stride, he walked to the back wall and inspected the rambling rose. 'Green-fly,' he shouted knowledgeably, looking up at the window. 'Riddled with green-fly.' It was Margaret's face at the window. She beckoned him to come upstairs.

When he came down the hall, Richard was standing at the front door with Dora. He turned and looked at Charles with disgust.

'I've been pottering about in the garden,' stammered Charles. He thought he might faint.

'Isn't it sickening,' said Richard. 'Someone's pinched the table.'

Charles stood on the top step and looked distressed. 'Where are the dishes?' he said, at last. 'And the glasses?'

'Gone,' cried Margaret shrilly. 'Every damn thing.' She put the kettle on to boil while Richard phoned the police. When Richard came back, Charles offered to jump in the car and drive in all directions. 'They can't have got far,' he said.

'He's already driven round the block umpteen times,' snapped Margaret.

Just as the tea was being poured out Malcolm strolled in and helped himself to the cup intended for Dora. He leaned against the draining board, stirring his tea with the end of a biro.

'Where have you been?' asked Margaret. 'You've been out for hours.'

'The park,' said Malcolm.

'Use a spoon,' ordered Richard. Shrugging his shoulders, Malcolm ferreted in the kitchen drawer. 'There ain't no spoons,' he said. His father ran up and down stairs, looking to see if his camera had gone or his cufflinks, or the silver snuff box left him by his uncle.

Charles and Dora couldn't stay for the arrival of the police. Charles said he hoped they'd understand but he didn't want to risk running into heavy traffic. Driving home to Tunbridge Wells, he told Dora he thought it had been a bit silly of Margaret to put the table in the front yard. 'I'm the last person in the world,' he said, 'to laugh at other people's misfortunes, particularly Richard's, but it struck me as affected, you know. Damned affected. I was right up against a dust-bin. Come to think of it, it was bloody insulting.'

'Why?' asked Dora.

'Well, I think she was probably poking fun at us. You know, lunch on the lawn ... that sort of thing.'

'Rubbish,' said Dora. 'She's just starved of sunshine.'

Charles felt awful. It was sheer worry that made him speak so spitefully of his friends. As soon as Malcolm had mentioned he had spent the afternoon in the park, he had realised how mistaken he himself had been about the noises in the basement. While he had sat at Richard's desk, the thieves had obviously been in the next room. He felt almost an accomplice. And those damned spoons lying in the yard – the police would think the thieves had dropped them. He could never tell Richard about it. Richard would be bound to ask what the hell he'd been doing in the basement. Even if it didn't occur to him for one moment that he'd been after old Margaret, he'd still think it odd of him to have been snooping around his desk. Nor, thought Charles sadly, could he confide in old Dora.

She was leaning trustingly against his shoulder, tired after her pleasant day, humming the theme song from *Chorus Line*.

5
Perhaps You Should Talk to Someone

We don't talk much in my family, according to my mother. We did when I was younger, she said, but after a bit it sort of died out. Evolution, I suppose. It's one of my mother's things, talking. She never stops going on about the importance of being articulate and communicating, but when you listen to her, it's just words. I mean, she's articulate all right but what she communicates isn't especially mind-blowing. Mostly it's pretty feeble, like being reminded to hang up clothes or put things away. When it's not like that she's pointing out how it's socially immoral to buy magazines with the money she gives me for tube fares. I might mention she uses the family allowance to buy cigarettes. Also, being progressive, my mother and father pretend to have this creepy belief in trust and privacy. Sad really. There's not much to discuss if they're not prepared to spy on you. Everyone I know with parents like mine, they all have to do the same. Keep quiet, I mean. What else can they do? 'I trust you ... I respect your privacy ... I would never dream of reading your diary.' They just allow you to get on with what you intended to do in the first place, but you tend to get this dreary guilt problem building up over nothing at all. It isn't as if many of us have got anything to be private about.

Actually my mother does read my diary, otherwise how did she find out I was having sex with William Hornby? As a matter of fact I'm not bothered about her violating my privacy. I mean, my mother doesn't have a thing to do after she's done the cooking and finished stuffing the clothes into the washing machine. I don't mind her having an interest. Anyway, I don't write the truth in my diary; most of it's made up. If you ask me, it's her that can't communicate. She's so screwed up about this trust thing that she's been rendered practically speechless except for muttering about tidiness and such like. She'd like to tell me to work harder at school but she knows it's a losing battle. After all, it was she who insisted that I should be educated by the State. She realises now that it was a crummy idea but she can't go back on her principles. My father says the same, but really it's because they can't afford it, and even if they could I'm so thick now that they couldn't get me in anywhere else. It's too late. It's not such a serious problem. I'm not alone. None of my friends have been taught anything either.

My mother really worries about not being able to talk to me. This summer she sent me away for a week to stay with an Aunt, just to get me away from William Hornby. She didn't say so, of course, but I knew that was the reason. Also, she's got a friend living in London called Moona who's divorced with one child by her ex-husband and another one by nobody in particular. That's probably a little too progressive for my mother, but she's known Moona for years and she's got this totally erroneous idea that I get on well with her. Actually, I don't mind Moona. She's pretty harmless. She sends postcards at Christmas of male statues without figleaves, and those ones of fat ladies in bathing costumes when she goes on holiday. She always writes a message about foreign parts. I've collected them all and put them in a box somewhere. Anyway, my mother said she'd write to Moona and I could go and see her when I was staying with my Aunt. 'You've always liked Moona,' she said. 'Perhaps you could talk to Moona.' I didn't mind either way. Everywhere's a bit deadly. You have to take yourself with you wherever you go. I suppose I could have told her that I thought William Hornby was a bit of a creep after all, and saved her the train fare, but what was the use? I couldn't summon up the energy.

I went to London and after a day or two Moona rang up my Aunt and asked to speak to me.

'Hallo, flower,' she said. She calls everyone that. I expect she thinks it's friendly. 'Why don't you come round and talk to me. I've got a letter from your Ma and there's a few things she wants me to ask you about.' Moona's got an odd voice, slightly clipped and a bit hoarse. She sounds as if she's heading for cancer.

I went round to see her. She lives in a big house in a terrace. The front door has two knockers on it, a plain black one and an ornate tarnished thing made out of brass. It's one of Moona's jokes. She always asks if you like her knockers.

'I'm in a bit of a crisis,' she said, as soon as she saw me. She showed me into the sitting room which has a sofa as old as the hills. When I sat down lots of dust went up to the ceiling. Moona's all right, really. Every time I've ever met her she's been in a bit of a crisis.

'There's this man,' she said. 'He's terribly odd. I can't fathom him at all. First he says he loves me, then he says he doesn't. He swore he'd come and see me today, but he won't.'

I didn't have to say anything; she wasn't really talking to me. She kept rubbing the side of her neck with her hand, the one holding her cigarette, as though there was something tied too tightly round her throat. I thought it was probable she might set fire to her hair.

Suddenly she asked, 'Have you got a boy-friend? A real one? You can tell me, flower. I won't breathe a word to your mother.' I knew she would; she wouldn't be able to help herself.

'Sort of,' I told her. I couldn't figure out what she meant by real.

'Are you in love with him?'

I stared at her and said nothing.

After a bit, she asked, 'Do you like him?'

'Not a lot,' I said.

She seemed bothered about something. I helped myself to one of her cigarettes.

'Do you smoke already?' she wanted to know.

'Sort of,' I said.

'When I was your age,' she babbled, 'I was in love quite badly. He worked for an insurance company. I can even remember his name.' She couldn't, not right away. 'It was Gerald ... no, Gerard – Gerard Carr. He was quite old. There was something odd about him. How old is your boy-friend?'

I said he was nineteen. Actually, that creep William Hornby is only sixteen. He doesn't even shave.

'I never liked young boys,' said Moona. 'It was always some friend of my father's that I got a crush on. They used to pinch my bottom.' She laughed quite loudly. 'What do you talk about?' she asked.

'Nothing much,' I said. I rested my head against the back of the sofa and closed my eyes. I felt sleepy. She was saying, 'I suppose it must seem strange to you that someone like your mother should have a friend like me.'

I didn't find it strange. I don't imagine my mother is the person she presents to me. I wasn't very interested. It's nothing to do with me.

Someone came into the room and I heard Moona say, 'Oh,

Bernard, you must meet Katie.'

I opened my eyes and this large man with brown hair was standing there. I think he wore glasses. Moona told me he was her lodger. She told him that I was the daughter of Agnes, her oldest and dearest friend. 'Agnes is a wee bit worried about her daughter growing up and all that,' she said. 'I do think its sad the way the young can't communicate with their parents. They always turn to those outside the family circle.' She did look dreary about it; it really seemed to bug her.

Just then there was a knock at the front door and Moona ran to the mirror and fiddled with her hair and threw her cigarette into the hearth. She suddenly looked stoned out of her mind. 'Oh, Christ,' she moaned. 'It's *him.*' She sort of sank into a heap onto the carpet.

'Steady up,' said Bernard. He sounded like one of those instructors at a riding school.

'Dear God,' wailed Moona. She was grinding her teeth and looking up at me. 'Don't ever wish,' she implored, 'for something very badly when you're young, because you just might get it when you're middle-aged.' I hadn't a clue what she was going on about.

Then she clutched Bernard around the ankles and begged him to take me down into the basement. 'Please talk to Katie,' she pleaded. 'I must be alone with *him.*'

'Right-ho,' Bernard said, and I followed him downstairs.

You could hear Moona greeting someone in the hall. Her voice was all breathless as if she'd been running for miles. I supposed it was her odd man calling after all.

Bernard was pretty odd too. He cooked some food and I lay on his bed and read magazines. Most of them had pictures in them of women without clothes. There was a lot of music and thumping about going on upstairs.

Two days later Moona telephoned and suggested that I

come over for lunch. We had chops and a salad and some bread that Moona said was Greek. 'How did you get on with Bernard?' she wanted to know.

'All right.'

'He's sweet, really. He pays forty-five pound a week for that basement and he's lovely with it. He was married once, you know, but something went wrong. We're very close but we've never had an affair ... isn't that odd? He's my best friend.'

I had thought my mother was her best friend. Possibly Moona has lots of best friends. It's no skin off my nose.

'Do you know what I did the other day?' she asked.

'No,' I said.

'Me and this odd man I'm mad about put on records and we danced. Did you hear us jogging about?'

'No,' I said.

'I'm sorry I left you alone with Bernard but I have been a bit unhappy lately and I did want to talk to this man and tell him one or two things.' She lit herself a cigarette but she didn't offer me one. 'I always feel better after I've talked things out ... don't you?' She looked at me and her eyes glittered. Maybe she was feeling weepy. 'You won't understand yet,' she said. 'You wait until you have children and fall in love.'

I thought at the time it was a weird thing to say. The children coming first, I mean. Actually, I never think of Moona as having children. They're always out at discos or gone hop-picking.

'Look here,' said Moona. 'Your Ma is a bit worried about you. She doesn't know how far you've gone.'

I helped myself to one of her cigarettes. She fidgeted and plucked at the skin on her neck. 'I mean,' she said, 'have you or haven't you?'

I kept quiet.

'You do know what I'm getting at, don't you?' she asked.

I shrugged.

'I can't think why she didn't ask you herself,' said Moona.

'She tried,' I said.

'And did you tell her the truth?'

'Maybe,' I said.

I don't see what it's got to do with Moona or my mother. I don't ask them what they do with men. I doubt my mother does anything, seeing she's got my Dad. Actually, me and William Hornby haven't done anything either. Nothing to write home about, that is. We used to spend hours in his bedroom listening to records, just sitting there. His hands used to shake when he changed the record. Once he put his hand on my jumper and I punched him. I don't fancy him any more. He's shaved his head and he's got a tattoo on his arm.

When Moona was washing the dishes she talked a bit more about her man. I didn't really listen. He'd bought her a book of poems or something. She'd bought a new dress to go out with him later that afternoon. She showed me the dress. I said it was all right. She complained again that she couldn't fathom her man.

I lay on her bed while she busied herself getting ready to go out. *He* was sending a taxi for her. She had a bath and came back wrapped in a blue towel. She looked a hundred years old. The skin at the tops of her arms was all loose. When she was ready she didn't know what to do with me. 'I could give you a lift part-way in a taxi,' she offered.

'It's all right,' I told her. 'I'll go and talk to Bernard.'

When she had gone I looked about for cigarettes but there weren't any. I read a letter in a drawer from some man who wanted to tweak her nipples. It wasn't very well written; it was about the same standard as a letter from that creep William Hornby. I went down to the basement.

'Oh, it's you again,' said Bernard.

I lay on his bed and after a time he lay down too. He didn't touch me; he just lay there with his arms at his sides and his eyes wide open staring at the ceiling. It was raining somewhere. You could hear water trickling down a gutter. There were no traffic noises, no cups rattling, no clocks ticking. It was like being in a cave and as if there were no other people anywhere in the world; as if Bernard wasn't there either. Just me.

I didn't like it. I didn't like him being so quiet. I asked him to give me a cigarette but he shook his head. I don't know whether he meant he didn't smoke or that I couldn't have one. After a while he kissed me. I expected he would. You can generally tell. He was covered in after-shave lotion. William Hornby says that only creeps use after-shave. I thought that maybe, in between kissing me, Bernard might say something. But he didn't. It spoilt it really. There was a man I met in a cinema once, and another man last Christmas at a party. They asked me questions. They made noises. They wanted to know how old I was and all sorts of different things about me. I never answered them, but at least they asked.

I didn't want to stay in the basement with Bernard, not without cigarettes and nobody talking. I said I had to go now.

'Righty-ho,' he said.

I didn't see Moona again. When I went home my mother didn't have much to say for herself. 'Moona phoned me,' she said. 'I must say I was a bit ashamed. She mentioned you helped yourself to her cigarettes.'

Fancy Moona noticing that. I don't suppose Bernard told her anything about me. I feel sorry for both of them. Probably they should talk to someone.

6

Through a Glass Brightly

Norman Pearson went to the meeting because his neighbour's wife, Alison Freely, told him he ought to mix more. He was afraid that Alison's reference to the meeting was a roundabout way of telling him that he was taking up too much of her time, and instantly said that he had every intention of going, that indeed he had already made enquiries about it long before she had brought up the subject.

Two years before, his wife had left him for a career woman with a villa in Spain. He had never met the woman, but his wife had cruelly left a photograph of her in the suitcase on top of the wardrobe. He often took down the photograph and studied that unknown face, those eyes that had winked at his wife across a crowded room and spirited her out of his life. In spite of every effort, he had not yet adjusted to being on his own. He had read that single men were in demand at dinner parties and things, but though he had casually let drop, in conversations with colleagues at the office, that he was on the loose, in a manner of speaking, no one had ever taken him up on it, not even to the extent of asking him round for a cup of tea. Last February he had become quite pally with a divorcee in Mount Street – patting her dog, passing the time of day –

until she sent him a note complaining about the dilapidation of the party wall at the back of his house. It wasn't that he objected to sharing the cost of doing something about it, rather that he dreaded some cowboy builder mutilating the rambler rose that he had planted against the wall in happier times. Actually, his wife had planted it; lately, he couldn't rid himself of the superstitious thought that if the rose didn't thrive, neither would he. The divorcee was still sending him solicitors' letters, because of course they were no longer on speaking terms and even the dog ignored him. He had come to the conclusion that if there was a demand for deserted men, men on the loose, then it existed somewhere else, in exotic Islington perhaps, or Hampstead, and had not yet reached East Croydon.

The meeting was called to discuss arrangements for the Mary Street Carnival, and was held upstairs in the *Hare and Hounds*. The accountant from No. 111, who owned a typist and a photocopying machine, had sent out the notices. It went without saying that his close friend J.J. Roberts, who was something controversial in the television world, took the chair. Not that people were fighting for the privilege of being that involved; not any more. Mary Street had organised a carnival, in summer, for the past eight years, and those serving on the Committee usually ended up out of pocket. It was a headache trying to recuperate expenses once the Steel Bands and the Inter-Action Groups had muscled in on the occasion. Nor had anyone forgotten the year the Committee, accused of being too middle-class in its attitude, had been persuaded to join forces with the Youth Centre at the end of the street. The youth leader, who was called Sunday and was an ethnic minority, had talked the landlord of the *Hare and Hounds* into applying for an extended licence. Afterwards, a majority of the residents, particularly those who had suffered broken windows, had protested that it was meant to be a day for the children. There was no denying that the Carnival itself had been a great success, at least until eight o'clock when the Committee were counting the day's takings in the Church Hall. Then someone shouted out the word 'Fire!', and naturally they had all run to see what was up. They only went as far as the door. Even so, when they turned round the cash boxes had simply vanished into thin air. There were the usual reasoned arguments along the lines of shooting being too good for 'them', and, send 'them' back on the next banana boat, but nothing came of it. The accountant had gone so far as to have notices printed, which were wired to the lamp posts, promising forgiveness all round and pleading for the money to be returned anonymously. Needless to say, he never heard a dicky bird. Since then, the accountant and J.J. Roberts, accompanied by a minder from the Leisure Centre, had gone round the stalls every half hour collecting whatever had accumulated in the cash boxes.

Carnival Day had evolved out of a desire to beautify the street. The proceeds of that first event had gone towards buying, and subsequently planting trees along the edges of the pavement. This idea of environmental improvement was abandoned shortly after it was discovered that no one had taken into account the camber of the road. In no time at all the roots of the trees had begun to interfere with the drains, and the Council had to come round and uproot them – it came out of the rates, of course – and stick them back into huge concrete tubs that were an eyesore. Alison Freely had a tub right outside her house, which meant she couldn't park her car properly. She put poison in the soil and killed off her tree, but the Council said they hadn't the manpower to remove the tub. Now nobody really knew what the Carnival was in aid of, or indeed what happened to the proceeds. For many it was just an excuse to get rid of worn-out clothing and broken furniture.

At the meeting, when suggestions were called for, Mrs Riley the architect said what about a competition for a model of the street as it might be in fifty years time.

'Marvellous,' said J.J. Roberts. 'Bloody marvellous.'

Nobody else came up with anything quite as complicated, though the graphic designer from No. 89 attempted to persuade people that it would be a fun thing to paint their balconies in different colours. He said it wouldn't cost much and urged them to think of those sticks of rock one used to buy at seaside resorts: such colours – such luminous pinks and greens.

Betty Taylor, whom J.J. Roberts always referred to as Elizabeth Taylor, and who lived in compulsorily purchased property, said that it wasn't fair on people who didn't have balconies. A senior citizen, she had recently attended a talk given in the Church Hall by a member of the Women's Workshop and was becoming increasingly aware of the divisions caused by privilege. She said that if sticks of rock were only going to be distributed to balcony owners, then she would vote against it. The accountant told her that in his opinion balconies gave easy access to thieves, and she should thank her lucky stars she was without one.

It was then that Norman Pearson remarked that his mother had once been burgled in Streatham. The swine had taken her television set and the transistor radio but ignored her crystal ball on the mantelpiece. He was astonished at the reaction resulting from this routine, though undoubtedly sad, little tale.

'Fortune telling,' hissed Mrs Riley. 'Fortune telling.' The accountant beat at his thigh with his fist and laughed uncontrollably. 'Christ,' exploded J.J. Roberts. 'How bloody marvellous.'

The next morning, when they were both emptying rubbish

into their respective bins, Alison asked Norman how he had got on at the meeting. He said he had found it stimulating. 'That show-off Roberts was in charge.'

'Of course,' Alison said. 'Many others turn up?'

'One or two,' he said, and as she was going back into the house, called out, 'I'm going to tell fortunes.' But his words were lost in the slamming of her door and he was glad that she hadn't heard, because he had promised not to tell anybody, so as to be more mysterious on the day.

He collected the crystal ball from his mother's a week before the Carnival. She didn't want to part with it; she said it was valuable. In the end he almost snatched it from her, and was surprised at its weight. Though he looked into it for hours, even after he had drunk three-quarters of a bottle of retsina, he could see nothing within its depths but a milk-white cloud. Irritated, he shook it, as though it was one of those children's snow-flake scenes encased in glass, but still he saw nothing beyond that impenetrable mist. His own life, he thought, staring gloomily out at the bunting already strung across the street, was becoming equally opaque. Deep down, he blamed his wife, for if she had not been so flighty he would never have been in such a predicament.

Preparations for the Carnival began at eight o'clock in the morning. They were lucky with the weather, in that it wasn't actually raining. J.J. Roberts strode up and down in a pair of shorts, chalking lines and circles on the surface of the road, and pointing at the sky. 'Lots of blue,' he shouted optimistically, whenever anybody appeared on the balconies. When he saw Norman, he cried out, 'Looking forward to it, Pearson?'

'Rather,' said Norman, wishing he had the courage to go to a main-line station and take a train in any direction.

At one o'clock the merry-go-round, the slide, the racks of

second-hand clothing were in their alloted spaces. The home-made cakes, the bags of fudge and toffee, the rag dolls and the tea-cosies lay spread along the trestle tables. From behind each privet hedge wafted a smell of frying sausages and hamburgers, of kebabs roasting above charcoal. A man on stilts, thin arms held wide, stood like a pylon in the middle of the road. Hordes of little children, pursued by parents, ran between his legs, screaming.

The Lady Mayoress opened the proceedings, standing on J.J. Roberts's balcony and shouting through a loud-speaker. Norman was crouched at a rickety table inside a wigwam anchored precariously in the gutter. He wore a flouncey dress loaned to him by the accountant's wife, dark glasses and a Davy Crocket hat. No one had recognised him when he appeared in the street. He was straining to hear the Mayoress's words when some children pushed against the wigwam. The table collapsed, sending the crystal ball flying into the gutter. When he picked it up there were tiny hair-line cracks upon its surface. It made all the difference.

His first customers were a man and a woman, neither of whom had he ever seen before, and he was able to tell them that they were going on a long journey, somewhere hot, without vegetation.

'Good heavens,' breathed the woman.

Encouraged, Norman studied the scratches carefully, and, screwing up his eyes fancied he saw the marks of tyre tracks.

'It's not going to be all plain sailing,' he said. 'I foresee trouble.' He charged the couple ten pence and realised, too late, that he could have asked for fifty. He heard them outside the tent, informing someone that the crystal gazer was incredible, absolutely incredible. She had told them all about that documentary they had made for 'War on Want', when the crank shaft went and David, but for the champagne, would almost certainly have died of dehydration.

A queue began to form outside the wigwam. The noise, the jostling, was tremendous.

'Stop it,' Norman protested, as a youth with a plug of cotton-wool in his ear insisted on entering with two of his friends.

'There's no room,' he warned, hanging on to his Davy Crocket hat as the tent lurched sideways.

'Get on with it,' ordered the youth belligerently.

'Well,' said Norman. 'You've been ill recently, with headaches.'

'Rubbish,' sneered the youth.

'Earache, then,' said Norman. 'I see a tall man with very long legs. He's waving his arms.'

'Bugger me,' said the youth, all the cockiness gone from him.

'You were mugged,' said Norman confidently, staring at a wavy line that looked not unlike the handle of a teacup. 'Attacked in some way.'

'Gerroff,' cried the youth, recovering. 'I weren't attacked, you stupid bag. Me Dad hit me with a poker.'

When Betty Taylor came into the wigwam, Norman found himself telling her that she had not had much of a life.

'You're right,' she said. 'You're right.'

'You've never had it easy, right from a child.'

'No,' she sniffed. 'I haven't.'

'And I can't see anything better in the future,' Norman said. 'You're not one of Nature's darlings. I wish I could pretend otherwise, but the crystal ball never lies.'

Betty Taylor left the wigwam in tears. Norman felt dreadful the moment she had gone, and wondered what had made him so peculiarly truthful. After all, she had done nothing to him.

Nevertheless he enjoyed himself; it was simple once he'd got the hang of it. Nicotine stains on the fingers pointed to a death-wish, blood-shot eyes denoted too much dependence on the bottle, nervous laughter was a sure sign of inferiority. It was all a matter of observation.

Half way through the afternoon a woman in a white dress squeezed into the wigwam. She was coughing. 'You're supposed to be frightfully good,' she said huskily. 'Do tell what's in store for me.'

Norman looked at her face, at her eyes, and then peered into the crystal ball. 'Sometimes,' he told her, 'I find it's not altogether wise to pass on the information. It might upset people – some people – if the exact picture were given.'

'Oh, come now,' she said. 'You can tell me. I've paid my ten pence.'

'I see a house,' he said. 'It's painted white. It's not here ... it's somewhere abroad.' He glanced at her sunburnt arms and went on, 'You've only recently returned. You weren't alone.'

'Go on,' said the woman. 'You're awfully good so far.'

'This other person,' he said, 'is unhappy. It's a woman. Her surname begins with P, I think. Yes, it's definitely P.'

'What does this P person do?' asked the woman. She was holding a little fold of skin at the base of her neck, twisting it between thumb and forefinger.

'Nothing at the moment,' said Norman, 'that's the trouble. She used to look after someone, but then she walked out.'

The woman stared at Norman.

'I think it was her mother,' he said. 'Someone close, anyway. At any rate they took it badly. I see a station platform and a figure standing very near the rails. There's a train coming.'

'Oh, God!' said the woman.

'There's something else,' Norman said, 'something else coming through. I've got it. I've a picture of a woman lying down and someone bending over her, someone in a white coat. Is she at the dentist's, I wonder?' He took his time; he was sweating and his dark glasses kept sliding on the bridge of his nose. At last he said, 'The woman has a sore ... no, not a sore, more like a small lump just beneath her adam's apple. It's serious.'

After a moment the woman asked, 'Which one is it? The woman at the station or the one with the name beginning with P?'

'Ah, well,' said Norman, 'I'm only the projector, not the identifier. I leave it to those who consult me to work out whose life is in danger.'

The woman put a pound note on the table and ducked out into the street. Norman could hear her coughing above the noise of the Steel Band on the corner.

When it was all over and he'd been congratulated on his success – more than one member of the Committee asked if he was free next week for drinks, for supper – Norman went home, and removing the suitcase from the wardrobe took out the photograph and tore it in half across the throat.

The he sat at the table and wrote a note to the divorcee, telling her that she could pull down his wall whenever she felt like it. If necessary he would pay for the whole caboodle.

Life wasn't all roses.

7
Bread and Butter Smith

Whenever the Christmas season approaches I always think of the good times we had, my wife and I, at the Adelphi Hotel just after the war. When I say 'times' I wouldn't like to give the impression that we were regular visitors to the hostelry at the foot of Mount Pleasant – that would be misleading. As a matter of fact we only stayed there twice. Before and in between those occasions we put up at the Exchange Hotel in Stanley Street, next door to the station.

Though born and brought up in Liverpool, I had crossed the water and gone to live on the Wirral at the earliest opportunity – you did if you came from Anfield – but I was in the habit of popping over on the ferry each Christmas to carve the turkey, on Boxing Day, for my sister Constance. She was, apart from my wife, my only surviving relative. Leaving aside the matter of Mr Brownlow, Constance's house in Belmont Road wasn't a suitable place to stay – to be accurate, it was one up and one down with the WC in the back-yard – and as the wife and I found it more convenient to occupy separate bedrooms I always booked into an hotel. I could afford it. I was in scrap metal, which was a good line of business to be in if you didn't mind being called a racketeer, which I didn't. The wife minded, but as I often tell her, where would she be today if I hadn't been. She'd soon buck up her ideas if she found herself languishing in the public ward of a National Health hospital.

If it hadn't been for Smith, we'd have stuck with the Exchange and not gone on switching hotels the way we did. Not that it achieved anything; he always ferreted us out. I fully believe that if we had changed venues altogether and given Blackpool or Hastings a whirl he'd have turned up in the grill room on the night before Christmas Eve, wearing that same crumpled blue suit, as though drawn by a magnet. I don't want to malign the poor devil, and don't think I'm being wise after the event, but I always found him a bit of a strain, not to mention an aggravation, right from the moment we met him, which was that first year we stayed at the Exchange.

We'd had our dinner, thank God, main course, pudding and so forth, and the waiter had just brought us a bowl of fruit. No bananas or tangerines, of course – too soon after the end of hostilities – but there was half a peach and a few damsons and some apples nicely polished.

'Shall I have the peach?' my wife said.

'Have what you like,' I told her. I've never been enamoured of fruit.

It was then that this fellow at the next table, who seemed to have nothing in front of him but a plate of bread and butter, leaned forward and said to me: 'The waiter is doing what King Alcinous may have done to the storm-beaten Greeks.'

That's exactly what he said, give or take a few words. You meet a lot of loopy individuals among the educated classes, and at the time I mistook him for one of those. Loopy, that is.

I ignored him, but the wife said: 'It's a thought, isn't it?' She was nervy that far back. Once she'd been foolish enough to respond, we couldn't get shot of him. I'm an abrupt sort of person. I don't do things I don't want to do – never have – whereas the wife, long before her present unfortunate state manifested itself, is the sort of person who apologises when some uncouth lout sends her reeling into the gutter. Don't get me wrong, Smith was never a scrounger. He paid his whack at the bar, and if he ever ate with us it was hardly an imposition because he never seemed to order anything but bread and butter. Even on Christmas Day all he had was a few cuts of the breast and his regular four slices. He wasn't thin either. He had more of a belly on him than me, and he looked well into his fifties, which I put down to his war experiences. He was in the desert, or so he told the wife, and once saw Rommel through field glasses.

All along, I made no bones about my feelings for Smith. That first night, when he intruded over the fruit, I turned my face away. Later on, whenever he began pestering us about the Maginot line, or the Wife of Andros, or his daft theory that the unknown soldier was very probably a woman who had been scurrying along the hedgerows looking for hens' eggs when a shell had blown her to pieces at Ypres, I just got to my feet and walked away. My wife brought it on herself. She shouldn't have sat like patience on a monument, listening to the fool, her left eyelid twitching the way it does when she's out of her depth. His conversation was right over her head.

Not that he seemed to notice; he couldn't get enough of us. When we said we wouldn't be available on Boxing Day, he even hinted that we might take him along to Belmont Road. I was almost tempted to take him up on it. Mr Brownlow was argumentative and had a weak bladder. Constance had picked him up outside the Co-op in 1931. It would have served Smith right to have had to sit for six hours in Constance's front parlour, two lumps of coal in the grate, one glass of port and lemon to last the night, and nothing by way of entertainment beyond escorting Mr Brownlow down the freezing back-yard to the WC.

The following year, to avoid the possibility of bumping into Smith, we went to the Adelphi. And damn me, he was there. There was a dance on Christmas Eve in the main lounge, and I'll never forget how he and the wife began in a melancholy and abstracted manner to circle the floor, her black dress rustling as she moved, and he almost on tiptoe because he was shorter than her. Every time he fox-trotted the wife in my direction he gave an exaggerated little start of surprise, as though I was the last person he expected to see. When he fetched her back to the table, he said, 'I do hope you have no objection to my dancing with your lady wife. I wouldn't like to give offence.'

'No offence taken,' I said. I've never seen the point of dancing. 'Do as you please.'

'We shall, we shall,' the wife said, laughing in that way she has.

We had to play cards with the blighter on Christmas Day. On Boxing Day it was almost a relief, which was saying something, to travel out on the tram to Anfield for the festivities with Constance and Mr Brownlow.

The next year we tried the Exchange again, never thinking that lightning would strike twice, or three times for that matter but, blow me, it did. Smith turned up an hour after we arrived. I did briefly begin to wonder who was avoiding who, but it was obvious that he was as pleased as punch to see us.

'My word,' he cried out. 'This is nice. My word, it is.'

I sensed he was different. There was nothing I could put my finger on; his suit was the same and he still blinked a lot, but something had changed in him. I mentioned as much to the wife. 'He's different, don't you think?' I said.

'Different?' she said.

'Cocky,' I said. 'If you know what I mean?'

'I don't,' she said.

'Something in the eye,' I insisted.

But she wouldn't have it.

All the same, I was right. Why, he even had the blithering nerve to give me a present, wrapped up in coloured paper with one of those damn soft bows on the top. It was a book on golf, which was a lucky choice, inspired almost, as I'd only taken up the game a few months before. I didn't run amok showing my gratitude, nor did I scamper upstairs and parcel up one of the handkerchiefs the wife had given to me. To be frank, I didn't even say thank you.

I didn't need acquaintances, then. As long as I had the wife sitting there, reading a library book and smoking one of her Craven A cigarettes, I didn't have to go to the bother of being pleasant. Not that Smith noticed my lack of enthusiasm for his company. It appeared to me that no matter where I was, whether in the corridor minding my own business, or coming out of the lift, or having a quiet drink in the Steve Donoghue Bar, he was forever bobbing up alongside me, or behind me – and always a mine of useful information. 'Are you aware,' he'd ask, eyeing the beer pitching in my glass as a train rumbled out of the station below, 'that the first locomotive was so heavy that it broke the track beneath it?'

He didn't seem to know anybody in the city, but a couple of times I saw him going down in the lift very late at night with his hat and coat on. God knows where he was off to. Once, I saw him in the deserted booking-hall of the station. I was on the fourth floor of the hotel, in the small hours, looking out of the back windows at the arched roof beneath, estimating what price, per ton, the cast-iron ribs would fetch on the scrap market. It was raining and Smith was perambulating up and down, hatless, holding an umbrella in a cock-eyed way, followed by a flock of pigeons. While I was watching, Smith suddenly spun round and flourished his brolly at the pigeons. I took it that he was drunk. The birds flapped upwards in alarm. There wasn't a pane of glass left intact in the roof – it had all been blasted to smithereens during the blitz. One of the pigeons in attempting to escape through the ribs must have severed a wing on the shards of glass. It sort of staggered in mid-air and then dropped like a lump of mud to the granite floor of the booking-hall. I couldn't hear the noise it made, flopping down like that, but it obviously gave Smith quite a turn. He froze, his gamp held out to one side like some railway guard waiting to lower his flag for a train to depart. I couldn't see his face because I was looking down on him, but I could tell by the stance of the man, one foot turned inwards, one arm stuck outwards, that he was frightened. Then he took a running kick at the thing on the ground and sent it skidding against the base of the tobacco kiosk. After a moment he went over to the kiosk and squatted down. He stayed like that for some time, rocking backwards and forwards on his haunches. Then he took out his handkerchief, laid it over the pigeon, and walked away. He was definitely drunk.

That final year, 1949, I switched back to the Adelphi. You've never clapped eyes on anything like that hotel. It's built like a Cunarder. Whenever I lurched through the revolving doors into the lobby, I never thought I'd disembark until I'd crossed the Atlantic. The lounge is the size of a dry dock; there are little balconettes running the entire length of it, fronted by ornamental grilles. Sometimes, if the staff dropped a nickel-plated teapot in the small kitchen behind the rostrum, I imagined we'd struck an iceberg. I never used to think like that until Smith put his oar in. It was he who said that all big hotels were designed to resemble ocean liners. On another occasion – because he was a contrary beggar – he said that the balconettes were modelled after confessionals in churches. I never sat in them after that.

7. Bread and Butter Smith

We arrived at four o'clock on the 23rd December and went immediately into the lounge for tea and cakes. I had just told the wife to sit up straight – there's nothing worse than a slouching woman, particularly if she's got a silver fox fur slung round her shoulders – when I thought I saw, reflected in the mirrors behind the balconettes, the unmistakable figure of Smith. I slopped tea into my saucer.

'What's up?' asked my wife.

'I could swear I just saw that blighter Smith,' I said. 'Could I have been mistaken, do you think?'

'What?' she said. 'You? Surely not.' She was lifting up her veil and tucking it back over the brim of her hat, and you could tell how put out she was; both her cheeks were red with annoyance.

The odd thing was that he never came into the grill room that night. 'Perhaps it wasn't him,' I said. 'Perhaps it was a trick of the light.'

'Some trick,' she said.

'If he has the effrontery to present me with another little seasonal offering,' I warned her, 'I'll throw it back in his face.'

After we had finished our pudding my wife said she was off to her bed.

'You can't go up now,' I said. 'I've paid good money to be here.'

'If I'm to live through the excitement of visiting Constance and Mr Brownlow,' she said, 'I'll need all the rest I can get.' She fairly ran out of the grill room; she never had any staying power.

I had a drink in the bar and asked the fellow behind the counter if he'd seen Smith, but he didn't seem to know who I was talking about. That's the trouble with shifting from one hotel to another – none of the staff know you from Adam. I looked into the smoking-room about ten o'clock and he wasn't there either. I could have done with Smith. The hotel was crowded with guests, some in uniform, full of the Christmas spirit and anxious that everyone should join in. Several times I was almost drawn into one of those conversations about what branch of the services I'd been in during the hostilities. I'll say that much for Smith; he never asked me what I'd done in the war. At a quarter past ten I went into the lounge and ordered myself another drink. There weren't too many people in there. A dance was in progress in the French room; I could hear the band playing some number made popular by Carmen Miranda. The waiter had just set my glass down in front of me when the doors burst open at the side and a line of revellers spilled into the lounge and began doing the conga down the length of the pink carpet towards the Christmas tree at the far end. They wound in and out of the sofas and the tables, clasping each other at the waist and kicking up the devil of a noise. Mercifully, having snaked once round the tree, showering the carpet with pine-needles, they headed back for the dance floor. And suddenly, for a split second, before he disappeared behind the tree, I thought I saw Smith near the end of the line, clutching hold of a stout individual who was wearing a paper hat. The fat man appeared again, but I was mistaken about Smith. Oddly enough, he must have been on my mind because for the rest of the evening I fancied I caught glimpses of him – coming out of the gents, going into the lift, standing at the top of the stairs looking down into the lounge – but it was never him.

Shortly after midnight I went upstairs to unpack my belongings. My room was on the first floor and overlooked Lewis's department store. I'd changed into my pyjamas – such as they were – and was putting my Sunday suit on a hanger when I realised that my wife had forgotten to include my grey spotted tie among the rest of my things. It wasn't that I gave a tinker's cuss about that particular tie, it was just that Mr Brownlow had bought it for me the previous Christmas and my not wearing it on Boxing Day would undoubtedly cause an uproar.

I went out into the corridor, determined to ask the wife what she meant by it. It wasn't as if she had a lot on her mind. Unfortunately, I forgot that the door was self-locking and it shut behind me. I rapped on my wife's door for what seemed like hours. I've never seen the point of chucking money away on pyjamas; the draw-string had gone from the trousers and there wasn't one button left on the jacket. When my wife finally deigned to open up, she too stepped over the threshold, and in an instant her door had slammed shut as well. I admit I lost my head. I ran up and down, swearing, trying to find a broom cupboard to hide in; any moment those blighters from the French room could have come prancing along the corridor.

'Fetch a porter,' advised my wife.

'Not like this,' I shouted. 'I'm not fit.'

'Here,' she said, and she took off her dressing-gown – it had white fur round the sleeves – and handed it to me.

I had crept half way down the stairs when I heard carol singing one floor below. I just couldn't face anyone, not wearing that damn-fool dressing-gown and my trousers at half mast. I hopped back upstairs and at that moment the wife called out to me from the doorway of her room; apparently her door hadn't been locked after all.

I spent an uncomfortable night in the wife's bed – I don't sleep well – and when I switched on the light to see if I could find anything to read, there was only the Bible. The room was a pig-sty; she hadn't emptied her suitcase or hung anything up, and there was a slice of buttered bread on top of her fox fur. I woke her and asked if she had a library book handy.

'For God's sake,' she said. 'I'm worn out.'

I was having afternoon tea the following day, on my own – the wife had gone window-shopping in Bold Street – when Smith arrived at the hotel. He said a relative had been taken ill and he'd had to visit them in hospital. Being Smith, he couldn't leave it at that. He had to give me a lecture on some damn-fool theory of his that we thought ourselves into illnesses. Our minds, he said, controlled our bodies. Some blasted Greek or other had known it centuries ago.

Faced with him, and realising that he'd be dogging my footsteps for the next forty-eight hours, I grew irritated. Don't forget, I hadn't had much sleep, and there was some sort of expression on his face, some sort of light in his eyes that annoyed me. I don't know how to explain it; he looked foolish, almost happy and it rubbed me up the wrong way. I wanted to get rid of him once and for all. It was no use insulting the man; I had done that often enough and it was like water off a duck's back. Then an idea came to me. I had recognised right from the beginning that he was a prudish sort of fellow. I knew that he had never married, and I had never seen him strike up a conversation with an unescorted woman, apart from the wife. He preferred the company of married couples, providing they were respectable.

'Blow me down,' I said. 'I've been getting pains in my legs for the past eight years. Now I know why.'

'Why?' he asked.

'On account of the wife,' I said.

'Your wife?' he said, tugging at his little ginger moustache.

I implied that the wife had led me something of a dance. She was under the doctor for it, of course. It had gone on for years. She couldn't be blamed, not exactly. That's why I was forced to keep changing hotels ... there had been various incidents of a somewhat scandalous nature with various men. As I spoke I stumbled over the words – I knew he wasn't a complete fool. I expressed the hope that he wouldn't betray my confidences. I didn't feel bad telling lies about my wife. It wouldn't get back. There was no danger of Smith repeating it to somebody he knew, who might repeat it to somebody we knew, because none of us knew anybody. It shut him up all right. The light went out of his eyes.

At seven o'clock that evening, according to the waiter on duty, Smith came into the smoking-room and ordered a pot of tea. The waiter noticed that he kept clattering the ash-tray up and down on the table. When the tea was brought to him, he said, 'Oh, and I'll need some bread and butter if it's all the same to you.' While the waiter was gone Smith took out his service revolver and shot himself in the head. He died almost at once. He must have been more upset about his relative being ill than he let on.

We never went back to the Adelphi, or to the Exchange for that matter. Not because of anything to do with Smith, but because less than a year later the wife began to show signs of instability; in any case the following August Constance passed on and there was certainly no call to clap eyes on Mr Brownlow ever again.

One could say that my wife has passed on too, only in her case it's more that she's wandered out of reach. As Bread and Butter Smith might have put it: 'All the world's against her, so that Crete (alias Rainhill Mental Institution) is her only refuge.'

8

Clap Hands, Here Comes Charlie

Two weeks before Christmas, Angela Bisson gave Mrs Henderson six tickets for the theatre. Mrs Henderson was Angela Bisson's cleaning lady.

'I wanted to avoid giving you money,' Angela Bisson told her. 'Anybody can give money. Somehow the whole process is so degrading ... taking it ... giving it. They're reopening the Empire Theatre for a limited season. I wanted to give you a treat. Something you'll always remember.'

Mrs Henderson said, 'Thank you very much.' She had never, when accepting money, felt degraded.

Her husband, Charles Henderson, asked her how much Angela Bisson had tipped her for Christmas.

Mrs Henderson said not much. 'In fact,' she admitted, 'nothing at all. Not in your actual pounds, shillings and pence. We've got tickets for the theatre instead.'

'What a discerning woman,' cried Charles Henderson. 'It's just what we've always needed.'

'The kiddies will like it,' protested Mrs Henderson. 'It's a pantomime. They've never been to a pantomime.'

Mrs Henderson's son, Alec, said *Peter Pan* wasn't a pantomime. At least not what his mother understood by the word. Of course, there was a fairy-tale element to the story, dealing as it did with Never-Never land and lost boys, but there was more to it than that. 'It's written on several levels,' he informed her.

'I've been a lost boy all my life,' muttered Charles Henderson, but nobody heard him.

'And I doubt,' said Alec, 'if our Moira's kiddies will make head nor tail of it. It's full of nannies and coal fires burning in the nursery.'

'Don't talk rot,' fumed Charles Henderson. 'They've seen coal fires on television.'

'Shut up, Charlie,' said Alec. His father hated being called Charlie.

'Does it have a principal boy?' asked Mrs Henderson, hopefully.

'Yes and no,' said Alec. 'Not in the sense you mean. Don't expect any singing or any smutty jokes. It's allegorical.'

'God Almighty,' said Charles Henderson.

When Alec had gone out to attend a Union meeting, Mrs Henderson told her husband he needn't bother to come to the theatre. She wasn't putting up with him and Alec having a pantomime of their own during the course of the evening and spoiling it for everyone else. She'd ask Mrs Rafferty from the floor above to go in his place.

'By heck,' shouted Charles Henderson, striking his forehead with the back of his hand, 'why didn't I think of that? Perish the thought that our Alec should be the one to be excluded. I'm only the blasted bread-winner.' He knew his wife was just mouthing words.

Mrs Rafferty's answer to such an outlandish invitation was a foregone conclusion. She wouldn't give it houseroom. Mrs Rafferty hadn't been out of the building for five years, not since she was bashed over the head coming home from Bingo.

All the same, Charles Henderson was irritated. His wife's attitude, and the caustic remarks addressed to him earlier by Alec brought on another attack of indigestion. It was no use going to his bed and lying flat. He knew from experience that it wouldn't help. In the old days, when they had lived in a proper house, he could have stepped out of the back door and perambulated up and down the yard for a few minutes. Had there been anything so exalted as a back door in this hell-hole, going out of it certainly wouldn't improve his health. Not without a parachute. He couldn't even open the window for a breath of air. This high up there was generally a howling gale blowing in from the river – it would suck the Christmas cards clean off the sideboard. It wasn't normal, he thought, to be perpetually on a par with the clouds. People weren't meant to look out of windows and see nothing but sky, particularly if they weren't looking upwards. God knows how Moira's kiddies managed. They were stuck up in the air over Kirby. When Moira and Alec had been little they'd played in the street – Moira on the front step fiddling with her dolly, Alec on one roller-skate scooting in and out of the lamp-posts. Of course there was no denying that it had been nice at first to own a decent bathroom and have hot water coming out of the tap. After only a few weeks it had become unnecessary to scrub young Alec's neck with his toothbrush; the dirt just floated off on the towel. But there was surely more to life than a clean neck. Their whole existence, once work was over for the day, was lived as though inside the cabin of an aeroplane. And they weren't going anywhere – there wasn't a landing field in sight. Just stars. Thousands of the things, on clear nights, winking away outside the double glazing. It occurred to Charles Henderson that there were too many of them for comfort or for grandeur. It was quality that counted, not quantity.

At the end of the yard of the terraced house in which he had once lived, there had been an outside toilet. Sitting within the evil-smelling little shed, its door swinging on broken hinges, he had sometimes glimpsed one solitary star hung motionless above the city. It had, he felt, given perspective to his situation, his situation in the wider sense – beyond his temporary perch. He was earthbound, mortal, and a million light-years separated him from that pale diamond burning in the sky. One star was all a man needed.

On the night of the outing to the theatre, a bit of a rumpus took place in the lift. It was occasioned by Moira's lad, Wayne, jabbing at all the control buttons and giving his grandmother a turn.

Alec thumped Wayne across the ear and Charles Henderson flared up. 'There was no cause to do that,' he shouted, though indeed there had been. Wayne was a shocking kiddie for fiddling with things.

'Belt up, Charlie,' ordered Alec.

Alec drove them to the Empire theatre in his car. It wasn't a satisfactory arrangement as far as Charles Henderson was concerned but he had no alternative. The buses came and went as they pleased. He was forced to sit next to Alec because he couldn't stand being parked in the back with the children and neither Moira nor Mrs Henderson felt it was safe in the passenger seat. Not with Alec at the wheel. Every time Alec accelerated going round a corner, Charles Henderson was swung against his son's shoulder.

'Get over, can't you?' cried Alec. 'Stop leaning on me, Charlie.'

When they passed the end of the street in which they had lived a decade ago, Mrs Henderson swivelled in her seat and remarked how changed it was, oh how changed. All those houses knocked down, and for what? Alec said that in his opinion it was good riddance to bad rubbish. The whole area had never been anything but a slum.

'Perhaps you're right, son,' said Mrs Henderson. But she was pandering to him.

Charles Henderson was unwise enough to mention times gone by. He was talking to his wife. 'Do you remember all the men playing football in the street after work?'

'I do,' she said.

'And using the doorway of the Lune Laundry for a goal-post? It was like living in a village, wasn't it?'

'A village,' hooted Alec. 'With a tobacco warehouse and a brewery in the middle of it? Some village.'

'We hunted foxes in the field behind the public house,' reminisced Charles Henderson. 'And we went fishing in the canal.'

'You did. You were never at home,' said Mrs Henderson, without rancour.

'What field?' scoffed Alec. 'What canal?'

'There was a time,' said Charles Henderson, 'when we snared rabbits every Saturday and had them for Sunday dinner. I tell no lies. You might almost say we lived off the land.'

'Never-Never land, more like,' sneered Alec, and he drove, viciously, the wrong way down a one way street.

When they got to the town centre he made them all get out and stand about in the cold while he manoeuvred the Mini backwards and forwards in the underground car park. He cursed and gesticulated.

'Behave yourself,' shouted Charles Henderson, and he strode in front of the bonnet and made a series of authoritative signals. Alec deliberately drove the car straight at him.

'Did you see what that madman did?' Charles Henderson asked his wife. 'He ran over my foot.'

'You're imagining things,' said Mrs Henderson, but when

he looked down he saw quite clearly the tread of the tyre imprinted upon the Cherry Blossom shine of his Sunday left shoe.

When the curtain went up, he was beginning to feel the first twinges of his indigestion coming on again. It wasn't to be wondered at all that swopping of seats because Moira had a tall bloke sitting in front of her, and the kiddies tramping back and forth to the toilet, not to mention the carry-on over parking the car. At least he hadn't got Alec sitting next to him. He found the first act of *Peter Pan* a bit of a mystery. It was very old-fashioned and cosy. He supposed they couldn't get a real dog to play the part. Some of the scenery could do with a lick of paint. He didn't actually laugh out loud when Mr Darling complained that nobody coddled him – oh no, why should they, seeing he was only the bread-winner – but he did grunt sardonically; Mrs Henderson nudged him sharply with her elbow. He couldn't for the life of him make out who or what Tinkerbell was, beyond being a sort of glow-worm bobbing up and down on the nursery wall, until Wendy had her hair pulled for wanting Peter to kiss her, and then he more or less guessed Tinkerbell was a female. It was a bit suggestive, all that. And at the end of the first scene when they all flew out of the window, something must have gone wrong with the wires because one of the children never got off the ground. They brought the curtain down fast. Wayne was yawning his head off.

During Acts Two and Three, Charles Henderson dozed. He was aware of loud noises and children screaming in a bloodthirsty fashion. He hoped Wayne wasn't having one of his tantrums. It was confusing for him. He was dreaming he was fishing in the canal for tiddlers and a damn big crocodile crawled up the bank with a clock ticking inside it. Then he heard a drum beating and a voice cried out 'To die will be an awfully big adventure.' He woke up then with a start. He had a pain in his arm.

In the interval they retired to the bar, Moira and himself and Alec. Mrs Henderson stayed with the kiddies, to give Moira a break. Alec paid for a round of drinks. 'Are you enjoying it then, Charlie?' he asked.

'It's a bit loud for me,' said Charles Henderson. 'But I see what you mean about it being written on different levels.'

'You do surprise me,' said Alec. 'I could have sworn you slept through most of it.'

Moira said little Tracy was terrified of the crocodile but she loved the doggie.

'Some doggie,' muttered Charles Henderson. 'I could smell the moth balls.'

'But Wayne thinks it's lovely,' said Moira. 'He's really engrossed.'

'I could tell,' Charles Henderson said. 'They must have heard him yawning in Birkenhead.'

'It's one of his signs,' defended Moira. 'Yawning. He always yawns when he's engrossed.' She herself was enjoying it very much, though she hadn't understood at first what Mr Darling was doing dressed up as Captain Hook.

'It's traditional,' Alec told her.

'What are you on about?' asked Charles Henderson. 'That pirate chappie was never Mr Darling.'

'Yes it was, Dad,' said Moira. 'I didn't cotton on myself at first, but it was the same man.'

'I suppose it saves on wages,' Charles Henderson said. Alec explained it was symbolic. The kindly Mr Darling and the brutal Captain Hook were two halves of the same man.

'There wasn't more than a quarter of Mr Darling,' cried Charles Henderson, heatedly. 'That pirate was waving his cutlass about every time I opened my eyes. I can't see the point of it, can you, Moira?'

Moira said nothing, but her mouth drooped at the corners. She was probably thinking about her husband who had run off and left her with two kiddies and a gas bill for twenty-seven quid.

'The point,' said Alec, 'is obvious. Mr Darling longs to murder his offspring.' He was shouting quite loudly. 'Like fathers in real life. They're always out to destroy their children.'

'What's up with you?' asked Mrs Henderson, when her husband had returned to his seat.

'That Alec,' hissed Charles Henderson. 'He talks a load of codswallop. I'd like to throttle him.'

During Act Four Charles Henderson asked his wife for a peppermint. His indigestion was fearsome. Mrs Henderson told him to shush. She too seemed engrossed in the pantomime. Wayne was sitting bolt upright. Charles Henderson tried to concentrate. He heard some words but not others. The lost boys were going back to their Mums, that much he gathered. Somebody called Tiger Lily had come into it. And Indians were beating tom-toms. His heart was beating so loudly that it was a wonder Alec didn't fly off the handle and order him to keep quiet. Wendy had flown off with the boys, jerkily, and Peter was asleep. It was odd how it was all to do with flying. That Tinkerbell person was flashing about among the cloth trees. He had the curious delusion that if he stood up on his seat, he too might soar up into the gallery. It was a daft notion because when he tried to shift his legs they were as heavy as lead. Mrs Darling would be pleased to see the kiddies again. She must have gone through hell. He remembered the time Alec had come home half an hour late from the Cubs – the length of those minutes, the depth of that fear. It didn't matter what his feelings had been towards Alec for the last ten years. He didn't think you were supposed to feel much for grown-up children. He had loved little Alec, now a lost boy, and that was enough.

Something dramatic was happening on stage. Peter had woken up and was having a disjointed conversation with Tinkerbell, something to do with cough mixture and poison. *Tink, you have drunk my medicine ... it was poisoned and you drank it to save my life ... Tink dear, are you dying?* ... The tiny star that was Tinkerbell began to flicker. Charles Henderson could hear somebody sobbing. He craned sideways to look down the row and was astonished to see that his grandson was wiping at his eyes with the back of his sleeve. Fancy Wayne, a lad who last year had been caught dangling a hamster on a piece of string from a window on the fourteenth floor of the flats, crying about a light going out. Peter Pan was advancing towards the audience, his arms flung wide. *Her voice is so low I can hardly hear what she is saying. She says ... she says she thinks she could get well again if children believed in fairies. Say quick that you believe. If you believe, clap your hands. Clap your hands and Tinkerbell will live.*

At first the clapping was muted, apologetic. Tinkerbell was reduced to a dying spark quivering on the dusty floorboards of the stage. Charles Henderson's own hands were clasped to his chest. There was a pain inside him as though somebody had slung a hook through his heart. The clapping increased in volume. The feeble Tinkerbell began to glow. She sailed triumphantly up the trunk of a painted tree. She grew so dazzling that Charles Henderson was blinded. She blazed above him in the skies of Never-Never land.

'Help me,' he said, using his last breath.

'Shut up, Charlie,' shouted Mrs Henderson, and she clapped and clapped until the palms of her hands were stinging.

9
Somewhere More Central

I never took all that much notice of Grandma when she was alive. She was just there. I mean, I saw her at Christmas and things – I played cards with her to keep her occupied, and sometimes I let her take me out to tea in a cafe. She had a certain style, but the trouble was that she didn't look old enough to be downright eccentric. She wore fur coats mostly and a lot of jewelry, and hats with flowers flopping over the brim; she even painted her fingernails red. I was surprised that she'd died and even more surprised to hear that she was over seventy. I didn't cry or anything. My mother made enough fuss for both of us, moaning and pulling weird faces. I hadn't realised she was all that attached to her either. Whenever that advert came on the telly, the one about 'Make someone happy this weekend – give them a telephone call', Mother rolled her eyes and said 'My God!' When she rang Grandma, Grandma picked up the receiver and said 'Hallo, stranger.'

The night before the funeral there were the usual threats about how I needn't think I was going to wear my jeans and duffle coat. I didn't argue. My Mum knew perfectly well that I was going to wear them. I don't know why she wastes her breath. In the morning we had to get up at six o'clock, because we were travelling on the early train from Euston. It was February and mild, but just as we were sitting down to breakfast Mother said 'Oh, look Alice,' and outside the window snow was falling on the privet hedge.

When we set off for the station, the pavements were covered over. Mother had to cling onto the railings in case she slipped going down the steps. The bottoms of my jeans were all slushy in no time, so it was just as well she hadn't succeeded in making me wear those ghastly tights and high-heeled shoes. I thought maybe the trains would be delayed by the snow, but almost before we reached the station it was melting, and when we left London and the suburbs behind the snow had gone, even from the hedges and the trees. The sky turned blue. I was sorry on Mother's behalf. You can't really have a sad funeral with the sun shining. She looked terrible. She looked like that poster for 'Keep death off the roads'. She'd borrowed a black coat with a fur collar from the woman next door. She had black stockings and shoes to match. She doesn't wear make-up, and her mouth seemed to have been cut out of white paper. She never said much either. She didn't keep pointing things out as if I was still at primary school, like she usually does – 'Oh look, Alice, cows ... Oh, Alice, look at the baa lambs.' She just stared out at the flying fields with a forlorn droop to her mouth.

Just as I'm a disappointment to Mother, she'd been a disappointment to Grandma. Only difference is, I couldn't care less. Whenever I have what they call 'problems' at school, I'm sent to the clinic to be understood by some psychologist with a nervous twitch, and he tells me it's perfectly natural to steal from the cloakroom and to cheat at French, and anyway it's all my mother's fault. They didn't have a clinic in Mother's day, so she's riddled with guilt. Apparently Grandma was very hurt when Mother got married and even more hurt when she got divorced. First Grandma had to go round pretending I was a premature baby and then later she had to keep her mouth shut about my father running off with another woman. She didn't tell anyone about the divorce for three years, not until everybody started doing the same thing, even the people in Grandma's road. Actually I don't think Grandma minded, not deep down; it was more likely that she just didn't care for the sound of it. There were a lot of things Grandma didn't like the sound of: my record player for one, and the mattress in the spare room for another. If we went down town for tea, she used to peer at the menu outside the cafe for ages before making up her mind. It drove Mother wild. 'I don't think we'll stop,' Grandma would say, and Mother would ask irritably, 'Why ever not, Grandma?' and Grandma would toss her head and say firmly, 'I don't like the sound of it.' And off she'd trot down the road, swaying a little under the weight of her fur coat, the rain pattering on the cloth roses on her hat, with me and Mother trailing behind.

Once I went on my own with Grandma to a restaurant on the top floor of a large shopping store. We were going to have a proper meal with chips and bread and butter. The manager came forward to show us where to sit and we began to walk across this huge room to the far side, towards a table half-hidden behind a pillar. My mother always moves as if she's anxious to catch a bus, but Grandma took her time. She walked as if she was coming down a flight of stairs in one of those old movies. She looked to right and left, one hand raised slightly and arched at the wrist, as though she dangled a fan. I always felt she was waiting to be recognised by somebody or expecting to be asked to dance. She went slowly past all these tables, and then suddenly she stopped and said quite loudly, 'I don't like the sound of it.' She turned and looked at me; her mouth wobbled the way it did when she'd run out of peppermints or I'd beaten her at cards. I was sure everybody was looking at us, but I wasn't too embarrassed, not the way I am when Mother shows herself up – after all Grandma had nothing to do with me. The manager stopped too and came back to ask what was wrong. 'You're never putting me there?' said Grandma, as though he'd intended sending her to Siberia. She got her own way of course, 'somewhere more central', as she put it. Before we had tea she smoked a cigarette. When she flipped her lighter it played a little tune. 'I don't like being shoved into a corner,' she said. 'There's no point my light being hid under a bushel.'

I wasn't really looking forward to the funeral. I'd been in a church once before and I didn't think much of it. I couldn't have been the only one either, because the next time I passed it they'd turned it into a Bingo hall.

When we were nearly at Liverpool my mother said if I behaved myself I could go to the graveside. 'You mustn't ask damn fool questions,' she warned. 'And you mustn't laugh at the vicar.'

'Are they going to put Grandma in with Grandpa?' I asked. I knew Grandma hadn't liked him when he was alive. They hadn't slept in the same bed.

My mother said, Yes, they were. They had to – there was a shortage of space.

'Do you know,' she said, 'your Grandma was madly in love with a man called Walter. He played tennis on the Isle of Wight. He married somebody else.'

I wanted to know more about Walter, but the train was coming into Lime Street station and Mother was doing her usual business of jumping round like a ferret in a box and telling me to comb my hair and pull myself together. She led me at a run up the platform because she said we had to be first in the queue for a taxi. We had a connexion to catch at another station.

It turned out that there was a new one-way system for traffic that Mother hadn't known about. If we'd walked, all we'd have had to do, she said, was to sprint past Blacklers and through Williamson Square, and then up Stanley Street and we'd have been there. As it was we went on a sort of flyover and then a motorway and it took twenty minutes to reach Exchange Station. She was breathless with anxiety when she paid the cab driver. We hadn't bought tickets for the next train and the man at the barrier wouldn't let us through without them.

'But they're burying my flesh and blood,' shouted Mother, 'at this very moment,' as though she could hear in her head the sound of spades digging into the earth.

'Can't help that, luv,' said the porter, waving her aside.

Then Mother did a frantic little tap-dance on the spot and screamed out, 'God damn you, may you roast in hell', and on the platform, echoing Mother's thin blast of malice, the guard blew a shrill note on his whistle, and the train went. I kept well out of it. The only good it did, Mother making such a spectacle of herself, was to bring some colour back to her cheeks. When the next train came we had to slink through the barrier without looking at the porter. On the journey Mother never opened her mouth, not even to tell me to sit up straight.

We weren't really late. My Uncle George was waiting for us at the other end, in his new Rover, and he said the cars weren't due for another half hour. 'Mildred's done all the sandwiches for after,' he said, 'and the sausage rolls are ready to pop into the oven.'

'That's nice,' said Mother, in a subdued tone of voice, and she leaned against me in the back of the car and held on to my arm, as if she was desperately ill. I couldn't very well shake her off, but it made me feel a bit stupid.

My Uncle George is an idiot. He said I was a bonny girl and hadn't I grown. The last time he'd seen me I was only six so you can tell he isn't exactly Brain of Britain.

It was funny being in Grandma's house without her there. She was very house-proud and usually she made you take your shoes off in the hall so as not to mess the carpet. My Auntie Mildred was dropping crumbs all over the place and she'd put a milk bottle on the dining-room table. There was dust on the face of the grandfather clock. Grandma was a great one for dusting and polishing. She wore a turban to do it, and an old satin slip with a cardigan over. She never wore her good clothes when she was in the house. My mother and her used to have arguments about it. Mother said it wasn't right to look slovenly just because one was indoors, and Grandma said Mother was a fine one to talk. She said Mother looked a mess whether she was indoors or out.

I wasn't sure where Grandma was, and I didn't like to ask. When the cars came I was amazed to find that Grandma had come in one of them and was waiting outside. There were only two bunches of flowers on the coffin lid.

'Why aren't there more flowers?' asked my mother. 'Surely everyone sent flowers?'

'I thought it best,' explained my Uncle George, 'to request no flowers but donations instead to the Heart Diseases Foundation. Mother would have preferred that, I think. She always said flowers at a funeral were a waste of good money.'

Mother didn't say anything, but her lips tightened. She knew that Grandma would be livid at so few flowers in the hearse. Grandma *did* say that flowers were a waste of money, but she'd been talking about other people's funerals, not her own.

I don't remember much about the service, except that there were a lot of people in the church. I thought only old ladies went to church, but there were a dozen men as well. At the back of the pews there was an odd-looking bloke with a grey beard, holding a spotted handkerchief in his hand. He seemed quite upset and emotional. He kept trying to sing the hymns and swallowing and going quiet. I know because I turned round several times to stare at him. I kept wondering if it was Walter from the Isle of Wight.

For some reason they weren't burying Grandma at that church. There wasn't the soil. Instead we followed her to another place at the other end of the village. The vicar had to get there first to meet Grandma, so we went a longer route round by the coal yards and the Council offices.

It was a big graveyard. There were trees, black ones without leaves, and holly bushes, and marble angels set on plinths overgrown with ivy. Four men carried Grandma to her resting place. Ahead of her went some little choirboys in knee-socks and white frilly smocks. They sang a very sad song about fast falls the eventide. It wasn't even late afternoon, but the sky was grey now and nothing moved, not a branch, not a fold of material, not a leaf on the holly bushes.

The vicar followed directly behind Grandma, and after him came my Uncle George, supporting Mother at the elbow, and lastly me and my Auntie Mildred. We went up the path from the gate and round the side of the church and up another path through a great field of grey stones and tablets and those angels with marble wings. But we didn't stop. The small boys went on singing and the men went on carrying Grandma and we reached a hedge and turned right and then left, until we came to a new plot of ground, so out of the way and unimportant that they'd left bricks and rubble lying on the path. And still we kept on walking. I don't know why someone didn't cry out 'Wait', why some great voice from out of the pale sky didn't tell us to stop. I thought of Grandma in the restaurant, standing her ground, refusing to budge from her central position.

After she was put in the earth, before they hid her light under a bushel, we threw bits of soil on top of the coffin.

I didn't like the sound of it.

10
The Worst Policy

Sarah made up her mind during Sunday lunch, after watching John help himself to his sixth roast potato. 'You shouldn't do that,' she said, as he poured yet more salt onto his plate.

'Hang it all, woman,' he complained. 'I've a big frame.'

As soon as he had gone out into the garden she telephoned her best friend, Penny. 'I've decided to go ahead,' she said. 'I thought you'd like to know.'

'Oh, Sarah,' said Penny. 'Are you sure?'

'Yes,' she said, 'we could all drop dead at any time.'

'*You* won't,' objected Penny. 'It's only John that's at risk.'

'My mind's made up,' said Sarah, and she replaced the receiver.

After tea she telephoned Penny again. John had gone into the living room to watch television with the children. 'What if *he* drops dead,' she asked, 'while we're in the middle of it?'

'It would be a bit awkward,' Penny agreed.

'If he actually went,' said Sarah, 'I mean actually in the middle I'd pull him off the bed and roll him under it until it got dark.'

'How would you be sure?' asked Penny. 'I mean, what would I do if he came to in the night and started moaning?

How would I explain it to Roy?'

'I've read about it,' Sarah said. 'There are certain signs. It's not just a question of holding a mirror to the lips.'

'I can't talk now,' whispered Penny. 'Paul's just come in.'

'Oh, *him*,' said Sarah crossly, and she hung up.

Paul was Penny and Roy's son. It wasn't a nice thing to admit, even to herself, but Sarah didn't like him. She had never taken to him, not even when he was a baby. As a toddler he had been a pest, and he didn't greatly improve as he grew older. Once he had torn all the heads off the carnations in her front garden – John was furious – and another time he told Roy's mother that Sarah and John had gone away for the weekend leaving the children all alone in the house. Roy's mother had actually rung up to check. Only two years ago he had used a pair of wire cutters on Sarah's bicycle chain. Of course she couldn't prove it, but she knew it had been him. His parents, if one was unlucky enough to run into him as he morosely entered or left the house, referred to his behaviour as absent-minded, vague. He never answered when spoken to and was quite capable of pushing aside anybody who happened to be in his path. 'He's a bit of a dreamer,' Roy often remarked. Both Sarah and John felt there were other words that might more accurately describe him, such as bloody-minded, self-engrossed and plain rude. Paul was now fourteen, large for his age and half way to growing a moustache. Irritatingly, Sarah's own son, Jason, admired him intensely, and, to her way of thinking, saw far too much of him. She was afraid that Paul was a bad influence; she knew for a fact that he smoked, and he still told lies. Penny called them 'fibs', but then she was his mother. Sarah herself was a stickler for the truth – as far as her children were concerned. 'Don't ever lie to me,' she would say. 'It's just not worth it. The truth never harmed anybody.'

10. *The Worst Policy*

It was fortunate that her opinion of Paul had not affected her friendship with Penny, for after twelve years of marriage Sarah had more or less embarked on an affair with Tony Wentworth.

Tony Wentworth was in the wine-importing business. He and Sarah had met at evening classes at the local primary school. Right from the beginning, when they both could tell that it was going to go further than it should, they had agreed not to bring their private lives into the conversation. Naturally, Sarah had slipped up once or twice, such as the time she couldn't help mentioning that Jason had just passed his cello exam, Grade II.

'Don't tell me,' Tony Wentworth had said. 'I don't want to know. And quickly Sarah had added that Jason was away at boarding school, in the country somewhere, and had been for years; she implied that she hardly knew him. It was a lie, of course, but then it sounded better, less adulterous, Jason being away from home and out of reach, instead of around the corner at the local comprehensive school and very much part of her life. 'I don't want to know about your past,' Tony Wentworth had said. 'The past has nothing to do with us.' It was a frightfully romantic thing to say.

Penny had met him too; she went to a different evening class but she'd seen him in the canteen. She'd spoken to him once and, though she couldn't remember in what context, she was sure he'd given the impression that he wasn't married. Talking it over, neither she nor Sarah particularly believed him. Recently, Penny hadn't been able to look him in the eye, not since she'd known about the affair. Every time she saw him in the corridor she turned bright pink, as though she'd spent most of her life in a convent. Not that it was actually an affair, not in the true sense, not as yet. Sarah telephoned her, sometimes twice a day, to talk about him. Penny didn't disapprove. She thought John took Sarah far too much for granted, and in a sense listening to the details of Sarah's love life was almost as much fun as having a love life of one's own. More fun in fact, because in time Sarah was bound to be caught out and, knowing old John, possibly dragged through the divorce courts, whereas she herself would remain happily married. Well, married at any rate.

'Have you seen him?' she would ask, whenever Sarah rang, and Sarah would usually reply that she hadn't or, if she had, that it was only for a few snatched moments dutside Woolworths or the Savings Bank. 'So it's not getting very far, is it?' Penny would say, and Sarah would have to admit that it wasn't. But then, as she rightly said, they had nowhere to go. Surely she was too old for thrashing about in the back of a car? 'You could come here,' Penny often told her – she was quite sure that Sarah would never dream of it – and then Sarah would go on again about what would happen if Tony Wentworth dropped dead of a heart attack while they were in the middle of it. Inwardly, Penny wondered whether Sarah gained some sort of perverse excitement from the thought of lying under a corpse. Or on top of one. After all Tony Wentworth was at least six years younger than Sarah, and looked as fit as a fiddle.

On Monday morning, as soon as the children had left for school, Sarah telephoned Penny. 'Well,' she said, speaking in a defiant tone of voice, 'what day will be convenient?'

'Oh, dear,' Penny said.

'You did offer,' Sarah reminded her.

'I know I did,' said Penny.

'Well, then?'

'I don't know what I'm doing this week.'

'Yes, you do. You always go to the hairdresser's on a Thursday.'

'So I do,' said Penny.

'And Paul has football practice.'

'So he does,' said Penny.

'Then it'd better be Thursday,' Sarah said severely, as though it was Penny and not she who was asking for the loan of a house for an illicit meeting that might end in tears.

They discussed what time Sarah should come round, and whether it would be better to have another key cut or to use Paul's key which was always kept under the plant-pot on the front step.

'Another one cut?' asked Penny, alarmed. 'Surely that's not necessary.' It was going to be difficult enough sitting under the dryer thinking of Sarah and Tony Wentworth bouncing about in her bed on Thursday afternoon without contemplating it on a regular basis.

'Paul *will* go to football?' asked Sarah. 'He won't bunk off?'

'He only bunks off school,' said Penny. 'Never football practice.'

She brought up the subject of Sarah's own children. Was it at all likely that they would come home early and finding her not there call round at Penny's house? Sarah said they had their own keys and, besides, Jennifer had ballet on Thursday and Jason his cello lesson.

'Well, that takes care of that then,' Penny said, and rather fiercely she slammed down the phone. In the afternoon she rang to find out whether Sarah had had second thoughts. Sarah hadn't.

On the Tuesday Penny nearly didn't go to her evening class; she didn't feel she could face Sarah, let alone Tony Wentworth. She felt she had been cast into the role of a procuress, a madame, though of course she wasn't going to take money at the door.

During the coffee break Tony Wentworth sat at a table in the far corner of the canteen with the fat girl who taught car maintenance.

'Have you asked him?' hissed Penny, shielding her face with her hand and speaking through clenched teeth.

Sarah nodded.

'And is he coming?'

'Yes,' said Sarah. She looked far from happy. Her face was pale and her hair, which was curly, seemed to have lost its bounce.

'It's not too late to change your mind,' whispered Penny. 'You could say one of the children was ill.'

'You forget,' said Sarah, 'I'm only supposed to have one child, and he's away at boarding school.'

'Tell him your husband's ill then.'

'I've hinted I'm a widow,' Sarah said, 'so he's already dead.'

'Well, tell him it's against your religion,' said Penny, and she began to giggle quite loudly.

'It's no use,' said Sarah, 'I've got to go through with it.' She looked gloomily down at her foot in its open sandal and jiggled her toes, as though they were gangrenous and amputation was the only answer.

When the bell went at the end of the evening Penny ran into the toilets and hid until she was sure Tony Wentworth had gone. She felt if she bumped into him she might make some suggestive remark, some obscene gesture; after all it was her bed he would be using.

She telephoned Sarah on the Wednesday. 'Sorry I rushed off,' she said. 'I remembered I'd promised to help Paul with his French.'

'I didn't notice,' Sarah said. 'Isn't it a dreadful day? I hate wet weather.'

'It's good for the flowers,' said Penny.

They fell silent, looking out of their windows at the roses

bending under the beneficial rain.

'How do you know Paul actually goes to his football practice?' asked Sarah abruptly.

'How do you know Jason goes to his cello lesson?' countered Penny.

'Jason's not a liar,' said Sarah and, stung, Penny put down the phone.

During the afternoon Sarah rang to apologise for being so tetchy. 'You know how it is,' she said. 'I'm so on edge.'

'I don't know how it is,' Penny said heatedly. 'I'm not in your situation.'

'Am I fat?' asked Sarah.

'You mean without clothes?' said Penny. 'How should I know?' And again she hung up without saying good-bye.

Sarah called round at Penny's house a quarter of an hour later. She was tearful and talked about the picnics she and Penny had gone on in the past, when the children were so little that they'd had to wear sun hats. And did Penny remember that time on Clapham Common when a dog had run up to little Jennifer and little Paul in his romper suit had toddled between her and the doggie, waving his chubby little fists and shouting, 'Go 'way, bad bow-wow.'

'I remember the time Paul ate all the chocky bickies,' Penny said, 'and you said one of them must own up, that the truth never harmed anybody, and Paul said it was him and your Jennifer went and bit him.'

'Oh,' whimpered Sarah, 'weren't they little darlings! What lovely days those were.'

Penny poured her out a glass of sherry and told her not to be such a fool. If she didn't want to go through with it, all she had to do was to say so. She, for one, would be relieved. What if John ever came to hear of it? What if Roy ever found out? Why, he'd probably insist on fumigating the house.

'Of course I'll bring my own sheets,' said Sarah, offended, and Penny gave her another glass of sherry because she was weepy again.

On Thursday morning Sarah telephoned to say that she would come round before lunch. Penny said, no, she wouldn't, that she didn't want her there until she herself had gone to the hairdresser's. The whole thing was somehow so deceitful, so calculating; she couldn't think how she'd been talked into it in the first place. She must have been mad. Roy didn't like people using his lawn mower, never mind his bedroom. The key would be under the plant-pot, and would Sarah please vacate the premises by five o'clock at the latest. Then she laughed; she was close to hysteria.

It was strange being in the house without Penny there. And even odder stripping the bed and changing the sheets; Roy's pyjamas were still under the pillow. Sarah had told Tony Wentworth to come at two o'clock, not a moment earlier and not a moment later. He believed he was coming to *her* house, and she'd invented a cleaner who left at a quarter to two in order to pick up a child from nursery school and returned on the dot of four o'clock. That way Tony Wentworth wouldn't run into Penny going out, or stay too long and catch her coming in. If the worst came to the worst, she told herself, she could always pass Penny off as the cleaning lady.

At ten to two Sarah was upstairs at the bedroom window, peering through the net curtains at the dusty little garden and the deserted road beyond the hedge. She had decided she would bring Tony Wentworth straight up the stairs. She didn't want him to see the living room; there was one of those spanish dolls on the settee. It was disloyal of her but she wouldn't like Tony Wentworth to think she was capable of choosing quite such a cheerful carpet.

He was on time and he brought her flowers. She had hoped

that he might have thought of bringing a bottle of wine. He was wearing a green sports jacket that she hadn't seen before.

'It's a fair-sized house,' he remarked, 'for one person.'

'I prefer it that way,' said Sarah. 'It's nice living on one's own. We'll go straight up, shall we?' And she led the way as though she'd been doing this sort of thing all her life. Which in a sense she had, only with her husband.

Now that Tony Wentworth was actually in Penny and Roy's bedroom, standing there with that bunch of chrysanthemums crushed against the lapels of his unfamiliar jacket, Sarah felt let down, tired. She longed to put her feet up and watch television. While she was undressing she thought of all the untruths she would tell if John asked her what sort of a day she'd had. It was wicked to tell lies.

She was lying awkwardly in Tony Wentworth's arms – they hadn't done anything yet; his skin didn't feel right and his feet were icy – when they both heard a scrabbling sound outside the window. It's a cat clawing at the drainpipe, she thought, and then there was a thump. Looking over Tony Wentworth's pimply shoulder she watched the window swing inwards and Paul clambering over the sill.

'Hang on,' he called out to someone on the path below, 'I'll let you in.' He crossed the room and went out of the door.

Tony Wentworth jumped out of bed and struggling into his trousers hopped in pursuit. 'Come back,' he shouted, 'come back, you rotten crook.'

Sarah sat there for a moment with the covers pulled up to her chin. Paul had seen her of course, or rather he had looked straight at her, as though she was part of the furniture. Surely he couldn't be that self-obsessed. She went to the window and looked down into the garden. There was a young girl in a mini-skirt staring up at the house. Then Paul ran down the path and out through the gate. The girl followed him to the bend of the road, until one of her shoes came off.

Penny telephoned that evening and complained that Sarah hadn't tidied up the bedroom. 'You left your sheets on the bed,' she said. 'And where are Roy's pyjamas?'

'In the dirty clothes basket in the bathroom,' said Sarah. She waited.

'Everything go all right?' asked Penny. Her voice was perfectly normal.

'I decided not to go through with it,' said Sarah. 'I'll tell you about it another time. I've got something else on my mind. Jason's not been going to his cello classes. He's been telling lies.'

'Oh, dear,' Penny said, 'never mind. They all do it. Are you going to let him see Paul tonight? He's expecting him.'

'I don't know how I can stop him,' said Sarah. 'It's bound to get out some time!'

'What are you talking about?' asked Penny. 'Are you all right? You sound terrible. Is it the lies? Is it Tony Wentworth that's depressed you? Is it the weather?'

'It's the truth,' said Sarah, and she hung up.

The truth, as she now realised, always harmed somebody.

11

The Man Who Blew Away

From the moment he arrived at Gatwick, Pinkerton began to be bothered by God, or rather by signs and portents of a religious nature. It was unexpected, and quite out of character, and he imagined it had something to do with suppressed guilt.

For instance, he was standing in the queue at the bookstall, waiting to pay for a newspaper, when the man in front of him turned abruptly round and uttered the words 'Go back'. The man wore a chain round his neck from which dangled a crucifix; it was easy to spot because his shirt was unbuttoned to the waist. And then, later, standing in line ready to check in his baggage, Pinkerton realised that he was encircled by nuns. They were not those counterfeit sisters in short modern skirts but proper nuns clad in black from head to foot, moon faces caught in starched wimples. Pinkerton was not a Catholic – if anything, he was a quarter Jewish, though he often kept that to himself – but he immediately felt unworthy at being in such sanctified company and stood aside, losing his place in the queue. It was then that one of the nuns distinctly said, 'It's too late, you have been chosen', and Pinkerton replied, 'You're right, you're absolutely right.' Then he shivered, because she had spoken in a foreign language and he had answered in one, though he had always been hopeless as a linguist and until that moment had never been vouchsafed the gift of tongues. At least, that is how it struck him at the time.

Thinking it over on the aeroplane, he wondered if there wasn't a simple explanation. The man with the crucifix had obviously not been urging him to return to Crawley but merely requesting that he should step back a few paces. Perhaps his heels had been trodden on. As for the nun, far from alluding either to life in general or to *his* life in particular, she had referred only to the passing of the hour. Possibly she had meant that there was no time to go to the Duty Free and buy *crème de menthe* for the Mother Superior. The business of his sudden comprehension of Dutch or German, or whatever guttural language it had been, was a little more tricky to explain. But then, hadn't he muddled it up a little and got the words in the wrong order? What she must have said, to a nun behind him, was *You were chosen* and then added the bit about it being too late, not the other way round. It made far more sense.

He had just decided that he had been the victim of one of those flashes of intuition which women seemed to be afflicted with most of the time, when he happened to glance out of the window. In the fraction of the second before he blinked, he saw a dazzling monster swimming through the blue sky, half fish, half bird, with scales of gold and wings of silver. He turned his head away instantly, and ordered a Scotch and soda. Afterwards he fell asleep and dreamed he was having a liaison, of a dangerous kind, with a woman who had been convent-educated.

At Athens there was some hitch in the operational schedule and he learnt that his flight to Corfu would be delayed for several hours. There was nowhere for him to sit down and the place was crowded. After two hours he gave in and, spreading his newspaper on the floor, sat hunched against a concrete ash-tray. Miserably hot, he was afraid to remove his sports jacket in case his passport was stolen. It would be all up with him if he had to turn to the British Consulate for help. They would very probably telex home and ask Gloria to describe him, and she, believing him to be elsewhere, would almost certainly say that it couldn't be him; disowned, he would be flung into jail. He had heard about foreign jails. A youngster in the office had been involved in some minor infringement of the traffic regulations in Spain and it had cost his widowed mother three hundred pounds to have him released. It was obviously a racket. To add insult to injury, he had been stabbed in the ankle by a demented Swiss who happened to be sharing his cell.

When at last Pinkerton's flight was called it was fearfully late. He arrived on Corfu in the middle of the night and was persuaded to share a cab with a large woman who wore white trousers and an immense quantity of costume jewellery. She was booked into the Chandros Hotel, which, she assured him, was in the general direction of Nisaki, and it would be a saving for both of them. It was pitch dark inside the car save for a red bulb above the dashboard illuminating a small cardboard grotto containing a plastic saint with horribly black eyebrows. The woman sat excessively close to Pinkerton, though in all fairness he thought that at the pace they were travelling, and bearing in mind the villainous turns in the road, she had little choice. He himself clung to the side of the window and tried not to think of death. Now and then, in response to something he said, his companion slapped him playfully on the knee.

At first, when she enquired his name and what part of London he hailed from, he answered cagily after all, he was supposed to be in Ireland, coarse-fishing with Pitt Rivers. But then, well-nigh drunk with fatigue, and dreadfully anxious as to what he was doing driving through foreign parts in the small hours, he found himself confiding in her. Talking to a stranger, he told himself, as long as it was in darkness, was almost as private as praying and hardly counted. With any luck he would never set eyes on his confessor again. 'I'm meeting a lady friend,' he said. 'She gave me a sort of ultimatum. I'm married, of course, though I'm not proud of it.'

'Of course you're not,' the woman said.

'Either I came out and joined her for a few days, or it was all off between us.'

'Oh, dear,' said the woman.

'Half of me rather wants it to be all off.'

'But not your other half,' said the woman. 'Your worst half', and they both laughed.

'I shouldn't be here,' he said. 'I should be sitting in the damp grass at the side of a river.'

'Of course you should,' she said. 'You've been chosen.' And she slapped him again, and he heard her bracelets tinkling as they slid on her wrist.

She was quite inventive. When he admitted that he was worried about being out in the sun – it always rained in Ireland in July – she said why didn't he come up with some allergy. One that brought him out in bumps.

He agreed it was a jolly good idea. 'I tan very easily,' he explained. 'On account of Spanish blood some way back.'

'You'd be best under an umbrella,' advised the woman. 'You can hire them by the day for a couple of roubles. Failing that, if you want to economise you can always hide in your room.'

They both laughed louder than ever because it was very droll, her confusing the currency like that. He would have told her about the allegorical creature outside the aeroplane window but he didn't want her to find him too memorable.

Upon arrival at the hotel it became evident that the woman was a bit of an expert on economy. She kept her handbag firmly tucked under her arm and appeared to have altogether forgotten her suggestion that she should contribute to the cost of the journey. He carried her luggage into the lobby, hoping that the sight of his perspiring face would remind her, but it didn't. She merely thanked him for his gallantry and urged him to get in touch should he and his lady friend fall out before the end of the week.

Pinkerton didn't think much of the Hotel. The fellow behind the reception desk had a mouth full of gold teeth, and there was a display of dying geraniums in a concrete tub set in front of the lifts. If he had not been so exhausted he would have insisted on their being watered immediately.

'I really must be off,' he said, and he and the woman pecked each other on the cheek. It was natural, he felt, seeing they were abroad.

'Don't forget,' she said. 'You know where I am. We don't want you coming up in bumps all on your own, do we?' And winked, and this time, his knee being out of reach, slapped his hand.

All the same, he was sorry to lose her. The moment he was again seated behind the silent driver his worries returned. What if there was an emergency at home and Gloria was compelled to telephone Ireland? Supposing one of the children had an accident and he was required at a moment's notice to donate a kidney? And what if Pitt Rivers' wife ran into Gloria in town and was asked a direct question? Pitt Rivers had boasted that though he himself, if called upon, would lie until hell froze over, he couldn't possibly speak for his wife, not with her Methodist background. How absurd in this day and age, thought Pinkerton, to be troubled with religious scruples, and he peered anxiously out of the window into the impenetrable blackness and watched, in his mind's eye, the roof of his half-timbered house outside Crawley engulfed in forty-foot flames. In the squeal of the tyres on the road he heard the cracking of glass in his new greenhouse as the structure buckled in the heat and his pampered tomatoes bubbled on their stems. It was so warm in the car that he struggled out of his jacket and rolled up his shirt-sleeves.

He had fallen into a doze when the car stopped outside a taverna set in a clearing of olive trees at the side of the road. For the moment he feared that he had arrived at the hotel, and was shocked at its dilapidated appearance. Not even Agnes, who was capable of much deception, would have described it as three-star accommodation.

A young woman sat at a rickety table, holding an infant on her lap. The driver left the car and approached her; Pinkerton imagined that she was his wife and that he was explaining why he was so late home.

In any event the young woman was dissatisfied. An argument ensued.

Pinkerton grimaced and smiled through the window, conveying what he hoped was the right mixture of apologetic sympathy. 'The plane was delayed,' he called. 'It was quite beyond our control.'

The young woman rose to her feet and she and the driver, both shouting equally violently, began to stalk one another round the tables.

'Look here,' called Pinkerton. 'I'm terribly tired.'

They took no notice of him.

Presently, he got out of the car and joined them under the canopy of tattered plastic. Yawning exaggeratedly, pointing first at his watch and then at the road, he attempted to communicate with the driver. For all the notice that was taken of him he might not have been there. Wandering away, he inspected with disgust various petrol tins planted with withered begonias.

He was just thinking that it bordered on the criminal, this wanton and widespread neglect of anything that grew, when the young woman broke off her perambulation of the tables and darting towards him thrust the child into his arms.

Taken by surprise he held it awkwardly against his shoulder and felt its tiny fingers plucking at the skin of his arm. 'Look here,' he said again, and clumsily jogged up and down, for the child had begun a thin wailing. 'There, there,' he crooned, and guided by some memory in the past he tucked its head under his chin, as though he held a violin, and swayed on his feet.

He was looking up, ready to receive smiles of approbation from the parents – after all, he was coping frightfully well considering he had been on the go for almost a day and a half – when to his consternation he saw that the man was walking back to the car. As gently as was possible in the circumstances he dumped the child on the ground, propping it against a petrol drum, and ran in pursuit.

The driver handled the car as if it had done him a personal injury. He beat at the driving wheel with his fists and drove erratically, continuing to shout for several miles. At last his voice fell to an irritated muttering, and then, just as Pinkerton had leant back in his seat and settled into a more relaxed position, the car veered sickeningly to the right, almost jerking him to the floor, and stopped.

Pinkerton tried to reason with the driver, but it was no use. The domestic crisis had evidently unsettled him; he refused adamantly to go any further. Jumping out of the car he opened the side door and dragged Pinkerton on to the road.

'I'll pay you anything you want,' cried Pinkerton, foolishly.

Three thousand drachmas were extorted from him before

his suitcase was flung out into the darkness, and the driver, taking advantage of his stumbling search for it on the stony verge, leapt back into the car, reversed, swung round and drove off at speed in the direction from which they had just come. Pinkerton was left alone, stranded in the middle of nowhere.

It was another hour, perhaps two, before he reached his destination. If he had understood the driver correctly, the track leading to the hotel was unsuitable for vehicles and dangerous for pedestrians to walk down at night, being nothing more substantial than a treacherous path between two chasms cut by the Ionian Sea. Remembering his days as a Boy Scout he had sat for a while on his suitcase, which he had retrieved from a clump of bushes so densely studded with thorns as to resemble a bundle of barbed wire, and waited for his eyes to adjust to the darkness. In time he saw the sky threaded with stars, but the earth remained hidden. He had wasted precious matches lighting his pipe and, puffing on it furiously, held the bowl out in front of him like a torch; to no avail. He had jumped to his feet and bellowed unashamedly, 'Help, help, I am Inglesi', and fallen over a boulder, bruising his shin. Finally he had sat on his bottom and dragging his suitcase behind him, begun laboriously to descend. Now and then, as the breeze shifted the branches of the olive trees below him, he caught a glimpse of a glittering ship on the horizon, and heard a roll of thunder as an unseen plane approached the airstrip of the distant town.

He was perhaps half way down the mountain when a curious light appeared above his left shoulder, illuminating the path ahead. Startled, he looked round and saw nothing. As he later tried to explain to a sceptical Agnes, it was as though someone was following him, someone rather tall, carrying a lantern. He was too relieved to have found what he took to be the means of his salvation to be frightened at such a phenomenon.

Soon the darkness melted altogether and he stood bathed in the electric lights of the car park of the Nisaki Beach Hotel. He climbed the shallow steps up to the reception area and only then did he look back. In the instant before the hotel was plunged into darkness he thought he saw a man dressed all in white, whose shadowy brow was flecked with blood.

The woman at the reception desk mercifully spoke English. She assured Pinkerton that the power cut was temporary and that it was not an unusual occurrence. She also said that it wasn't allowed for him to enter Mrs Lowther's room. It had nothing to do with the hour. Mrs Lowther was a package holiday and he wasn't included. She would rent him a room on the same floor, with twin beds, shower and use of cot. The latter convenience would be two thousand drachmas extra. Too tired to argue, and aware that the seat of his trousers was threadbare and his jacket torn at the elbow, he paid what was asked and, the lifts being out of order, borrowed a torch and toiled up the eight flights of stairs to his room on the fourth floor.

He was awakened during the night by a severe tingling in his arm. Finding that he was still in his clothes, he sat wearily on the edge of the bed and began to undress. The sensation in his arm had now become one of irritation; he scratched himself vigorously, imagining that he had been attacked on the mountainside by mosquitoes. Looking down, he was astonished to see a patch of skin on his forearm fan-shaped and topped by a pattern of dots so pale in contrast to the rest of his skin as to appear luminous. He tried to find the light switch so that he could examine his arm more closely. It was not inconceivable that he had been bitten by a snake, or even by a series of snakes, for he counted six puncture marks, though his flesh was perfectly smooth to the touch. Unable to locate the bedside lamp and not suffering from either pain or nausea, he fell back on to the pillow and slept.

Agnes telephoned his room the next morning. 'So you've turned up,' she said. She made it sound like an accusation, as if he was pestering her rather than that he was here at her insistence.

'I've had a terrible time,' he told her. 'You wouldn't believe it. First of all there was the plane journey, travelling all that way alone.'

'You mean you flew in an empty aeroplane?' she asked.

'You know perfectly well what I mean,' he said crossly. 'And there was a five-hour delay at Athens.'

'Stop moaning,' she said. 'I'll see you at breakfast.'

He shaved and showered and put on a clean shirt and the only other pair of trousers he had brought with him. He hid the woollen socks and jumpers, packed by his wife, inside the wardrobe and bundled his wellington boots under the bed. He hoped Agnes wouldn't spot them.

In spite of his experiences of the night before he felt amazingly fit, almost a new man. True, his hands were covered in cuts and scratches and his shin somewhat grazed and tender, but in every other respect he had never felt so healthy, so carefree. The view from his balcony – the green lawns, the flowering shrubs, the gravel paths leading to bowers roofed with straw and overhung with Bougainvillaea, the glimpse of swimming pool – delighted him. Beyond the pool he could see striped umbrellas on a pebbled beach beside a stretch of water that sparkled to an horizon edged with purple mountains. It was all so pretty, so picturesque. The whole world was drenched in sunshine. A tiny figure, suspended beneath a scarlet parachute, drifted between the blue heavens and the bright blue sea.

Even Agnes sensed the change in him. 'I thought you said you'd had an awful time.'

'I did,' he replied cheerfully. 'Absolutely dreadful.' And he helped himself to yoghurt and slices of peach and didn't once grumble at the absence of bacon and eggs.

He wasn't quite sure how much he dare tell her: and yet he longed to confide in someone. Agnes could be very cruel on occasions. Omitting only the words *You've been chosen*, he told her about the nun at the airport at Gatwick.

Agnes listened earnestly, and when he had finished remarked that she herself had often understood foreign languages, even when she didn't know any of the words. She'd met a Russian once at a party and she'd known, really known, exactly what he was saying. She thought it had probably something to do with telepathy. 'Mind you,' she admitted, 'the vodka was coming out of my ears.'

'Yes,' he said doubtfully, 'but I answered her. In Dutch as far as I know.'

Agnes agreed that it was odd; she looked at him with interest. She was frowning and he was pleased because he recognised her expression of intense concentration as one of sexual arousal. As far as he remembered she had never been excited by nuns before. Encouraged, he recounted the episode on the mountainside and his terrible descent.

'There's a perfectly good road higher up,' she said. 'It's sign-posted. It's only a hundred yards further along from that track.'

'How was I to know,' he said. 'It seems to me that I had no choice.' He described the guide dressed in white.

'No,' said Agnes. 'I can't buy that. It's almost blasphemous.'

'I'm only telling you what I saw,' he protested.

'But a crown of thorns,' she cried. 'How can you say such a thing? It's far more likely that you saw a fisherman in his nightshirt and one of those straw hats they all wear.'

'I know a hat when I see one,' he argued. 'I'm not blind.'

'It had probably been chewed by a goat,' she said. 'Or a donkey. You just saw the chewed bits, damn it.'

He attempted to change the subject and tell her about the baby at the taverna. Agnes was still aroused, though no longer in a way that would be beneficial to him. If he didn't watch his step she would lock him out of her room for days. 'It was a dear little soul,' he said. 'Quite enchanting, if a little pale.'

'Why the hell,' interrupted Agnes, 'would Jesus want to guide *you* to the Nisaki Beach Hotel? You're an adulterer.'

'An unwilling one,' he snapped, and fell into an offended silence.

He apologised to her that afternoon. She forgave him and consented to come to his room. When he closed the shutters the bars of the cot lay in striped shadows across her thighs. Her body was so dark after a week in the sun that it was like making advances to a stranger. He wasn't sure that the experience was enjoyable.

'Why have you kept your shirt on?' she asked him later, and he explained that he was perspiring so copiously with the heat that he was afraid she'd find him unpleasant.

'You are a bit sweaty,' she said, and wrapped the sheet round her like a shroud.

After three days he decided that he ought to go home. Agnes was behaving badly. He had run out of excuses for keeping out of reach of the sun and was tired of being insulted. When he lay in the shade of the olive trees Agnes snatched the newspaper from his face and complained that he could be mistaken for an old dosser. 'For God's sake,' she ordered, 'take off those woollen socks', and for his own sake he fought her off as she clawed at the laces of his shoes. All the same, he couldn't make up his mind when to leave, and lingered, dozing in his room or in one of those fragrant bowers in the pleasant garden. He still felt well, he still felt that absence of care which he now realised he had last known as a child. At night he put his pillow at the foot of the bed and fell asleep with his hand clutching the bars of the cot.

Towards the end of the week they went on an excursion into Corfu Town. Pinkerton said he wanted to buy Agnes a piece of jewellery. They both knew that it was his farewell gift to her. She pretended that it was kind of him. When she returned to England he would telephone her once or twice to ask how she was, perhaps even take her out to lunch, and then the relationship would be over. Something had changed in him; he no longer needed her to berate him, and she was too old to change her ways. He could tell that she was uneasy with him, and wondered if his wife would feel the same.

Agnes chose an inexpensive bracelet and stuffed it carelessly into her handbag. She said she was off to buy postcards. He offered to go with her but she wouldn't hear of it. 'You hate shopping,' she said.

He arranged to wait for her at a café in the square. She didn't look back, which was a bad sign. He wasn't at all sure that she hadn't gone straight off to hire a cab to take her back to the hotel.

Half an hour passed. He was sitting at a table at the edge of the cricket pitch, smoking his pipe, when a woman in a red dress sat down opposite him and slapped his wrist.

'Good heavens,' he cried, recognising the gesture if not the face.

'I owe you some money,' she said. 'My share of the cab fare', and though he protested, she insisted. She had also bought him a little present, because she had known she would bump into him sooner or later. She took an envelope from her handbag and gave it to him. Inside was a cardboard bookmark with a picture on it.

'How very kind of you,' Pinkerton said, and began to tremble.

'It's St John of Hiding,' said the woman. 'The saint of all those who carry a secret burden of hidden sin.'

Before they parted she asked him how he was getting on with his lady friend. He admitted that it was pretty well all over between them.

'I'm glad to hear it,' the woman said. 'I'm sure you're destined for higher things.'

Agnes saw the bookmark by mistake. When they got back to the hotel and Pinkerton was looking for money to pay the cab fare, he inadvertently pulled it out of his pocket. 'Why did you buy that?' she asked.

'It's a picture of a saint,' he said. 'A Greek one.'

'It's not very well drawn,' she said. 'One of the hands has got six fingers.'

Alone in his room he took off his jacket and laid it on the bed beside the bookmark. Rubbing his arm he went out onto the balcony and watched the scarlet parachute blow across the sky.

The next morning he told Agnes that he was leaving. He thought she looked relieved. He said that before he went he was determined to have one of those parachute rides.

'Good God,' she said. 'I mustn't miss this.'

She went to the jetty with him and watched, grinning, while he was strapped into his harness. 'Wonders will never cease,' she called out, as he took off his shirt.

He was instructed to hold on to the bar and break into a run when he felt the tug of the rope. When he was in the air he must hold on to the bar even though the harness would support him. He said he understood.

The speedboat chugged in a half circle beyond the jetty, waiting for the signal to be given; then, accelerating, it roared out to sea. Pinkerton was jerked forward, and gasping he ran and jumped and was swung upwards, his mouth wide open and his heart thudding fit to burst. Then he was riding through the air, not floating as he had hoped, for he was still tethered to the boat. He felt cheated.

The sudden and furious gust of wind that seized the rope in its giant fist and tore it, steel hook and all from the funnel of the boat, was spent in an instant. Then Pinkerton, free as a bird, soared into the blue under the red umbrella of his parachute.

Everything else that had happened to him, he thought, had a logical explanation; the nuns, the man who had come to his aid on the dark mountain, the woman and her choice of bookmark. Even the creature outside the aeroplane window had been nothing more than a reflection of the sunlight on the fuselage. Everything but that –

And before he blew away he looked up at that luminous imprint of a six fingered hand which was stamped on the flesh of his arm.

12
Helpful O'Malley

O'Malley let the girl into the house and showed her the room on the second floor. He had put the card in the tobacconist's window only that morning and already he had interviewed three people. Two had been career women and the third a young man who had laughed and joked all the way up the stairs. Neither the women nor the laughing boy had been right for the room. Of that O'Malley was sure.

Mrs Darnley, who owned the property and had returned to Dublin because the taxes were killing her, trusted O'Malley implicitly in the matter of tenants. He had a flair for picking the right people – solvent people who could be relied upon to pay the rent into the bank every month regular as clockwork. People, what is more, who when they moved on left the place as they found it, or, more often than not, in an improved condition. Not that any of them had wanted to move on – at any rate none of those occupying the ground, first or upper floors. They all said that they had been very happy in the house, that they would never forget their time in it. But for getting married, taking a new job in an another part of the country, or having an addition to the family, wild horses wouldn't have dragged them from the place. It wasn't an especially interesting-looking house: the plumbing needed overhauling, and keeping warm in the winter was always a problem. All the same, tenants grew attached to it, and many came back over the years, just to visit for half an hour or so, and sometimes they would spend the last five minutes standing in the front garden staring up at the windows, smiling at memories. There was still coloured glass in the fanlight above the door.

The letting of the second floor, however, had always posed a problem. Finding the right person was a constant source of worry to O'Malley. No tenant ever stayed for very long on the second floor; several had moved on in the space of a few weeks, and certainly none of those was ever likely to come back.

O'Malley had had the room redecorated three times in as many years, hoping to break some sort of pattern. He'd also taken it upon himself to choose a new bed, charging it to Mrs Darnley, and he had wanted to replace the old gas fire with an electric heater. Mrs Darnley had opposed the idea; she thought it would interfere with the character of the house. Besides, it would mean new meters. Perhaps he should lop off a few branches from the tree in the back garden, she had suggested, to make the room a little lighter, less gloomy in winter; but O'Malley had refused adamantly. He had spoken on the telephone to Mrs Darnley and told her he wouldn't hear of it.

'I'm only talking about one branch,' she had reasoned. 'Two at the most. Never the whole tree.'

'Over my dead body,' he said, and in the circumstances she had let the matter drop. O'Malley wasn't in Mrs Darnley's employ. He was a tenant, not a caretaker. He looked after the house and Mrs Darnley's interests because she no longer lived on the premises and he liked to be of use. He was helpful by nature.

O'Malley wasn't altogether sure that the girl was right for

the room. Wasn't she a little too self-possessed, a shade off-hand in the way she eyed the furniture, the new bed, the brand-new rug in front of the hearth? Didn't that sort often feel the world owed them a living and in the end do a flit with the cutlery and the bed linen stuffed into a haversack? Of course, she could be putting it on. Usually he could tell by their eyes whether they were suitable or not, but this one was wearing dark glasses. He couldn't tell a thing from her clothes. There were patches on her trousers and her shirt could have done with a wash. One of her shoes had a bit of string for a lace. But then, young Mrs Temple on the first floor wore jumpers with holes in them and she was the daughter of a baronet.

'Will you have it?' he asked, taking a gamble.

'I might as well,' the girl said. 'I suppose you want a month in advance.'

'That I do,' he said, and she wrote him a cheque, signing it 'Edith Carp'.

'Why is it so cheap?' she asked, standing beside the cooker and looking out at the tree. She reached up to pull down the window.

'It's nailed up,' he told her. 'It's an old house and the frames don't fit. We're not out to make a fortune, simply to cover costs. You won't find it easy to keep warm. There's a meter in the cupboard under the sink. It fairly gobbles up the money.'

'Is there anything else I should know?' the girl asked. Her tone of voice sounded insolent, but then he couldn't be sure, not without seeing her eyes.

'We shouldn't like you to bring anyone back,' he said. 'Not for longer than the odd night or so. It's not the morals we're on about. The bathroom's shared and it won't run to a crowd.'

'I won't be bringing anyone back,' said the girl. 'Not even for an hour.'

Then O'Malley knew that his instinct hadn't failed him.

Edith Carp was perfectly right for the room.

He left her alone for the first week, as was his policy. People didn't like being interrupted when they were busy changing the room to fit their personality. The girl before last had pulled down the curtains and hidden the engraving of the Death of Nelson under the bed, but he hadn't known that until her departure. And the girl before her had tried to put up shelves, bringing down a quantity of plaster; even though he had heard the hammering he hadn't knocked on her door until the week was out.

Not that Edith Carp made any noise at all. She evidently didn't own such a thing as a radio, and he was certain she hadn't bothered to rent a television set. She couldn't have brought with her more than two or three books at the most and he was at a loss to think how she spent her time, for though he couldn't swear to it he didn't believe she had been out of the house for more than a couple of hours since her arrival. Possibly she was sleeping. He didn't like to dwell on the possibility that she might be on drugs. That sort of problem was beyond him and he wouldn't be able to help her. Worse, she wouldn't need his help.

Edith Carp was so quiet that on the Thursday young Mrs Temple met O'Malley on the stairs and inquired whether he had managed to let the room.

'That I have,' he said.

'To whom? What sort of person?'

'A female,' he replied. 'Young and unemployed but with a bank balance. Her cheque has gone through.'

'And is she – all right?'

'I hope so,' he said, and crossed himself.

'Does she know? Did you tell her?'

'That I didn't,' he admitted. 'It would hardly have been an inducement.'

'Keep an eye on her,' begged Mrs Temple.

He assured her that he had every intention of doing so, and went on down the stairs to fetch the milk.

Still, it was easier said than done, seeing that Edith Carp remained so much in her room. She didn't pop out to borrow tea or sugar or the use of a bottle-opener, and though he waited she didn't come to him for instruction on how to light the antiquated geyzer in the bathroom.

Twice he stood listening on the landing outside her room in the middle of the night. On neither occasion did he hear anything of significance, nothing that couldn't be traced to the tapping of the tree against her window.

Shortly after lunch on the Monday he knocked on her door. She was sitting on the rug in front of the gas fire. The fire was unlit and the room was freezing. She was wearing a coat over her dressing-gown, and had left off her glasses.

'I just wanted to make sure,' he said, 'that you have two of everything – cups, plates – the requisite amount of forks.'

'There's only one of me,' she said listlessly.

The room was untouched. There wasn't a photograph on the mantelpiece or a poster on the wall. The bed hardly looked as though it had been slept in.

'I'm giving myself a party on Friday,' he said. 'The other tenants have accepted. Would you consider coming yourself? Just for the odd ten minutes.'

'No,' she said. 'I wouldn't.'

'I see,' he said. 'You don't like the look of me.' Raising his coat collar about his chin in an attempt to hide the livid birthmark which covered his face like a wrinkled rag, he left the room, closing the door meekly behind him.

He didn't doubt she would change her mind. Such a remark usually had an effect on women. First they experienced guilt, then pity; and later they felt resentful, which made them talkative. He couldn't help them unless he could persuade them to talk. That girl two years ago, the one whose young man had thrown her over after he'd found out she'd had an abortion, had been even more unapproachable than Edith Carp, and yet she had come to his party. It was different with men, of course. If the subject was raised, they generally skipped pity and guilt and jumped immediately into resentment. With men who needed help he never alluded to his disfigurement.

Edith Carp came to his room the following day. He was surprised at the quickness of her response. She wondered if she could ask him a favour? She wanted to move the wardrobe to the other side of the room and didn't feel she could manage it on her own. He said he was always more than ready to lend a helping hand.

Afterwards she insisted on making him a cup of instant coffee. He took his flask from his pocket and asked if she would like a small drop of whisky with her drink. She said she would. Neither of them imbibed all that much.

She told him that she had rented the room to get away from her mother who was dying of cancer.

He wasn't sure it was the truth, but then he'd been wrong before and so kept an open mind.

It was wrong of her, she said, but she hadn't been able to stand it. 'I can't bear the way she looks any more,' she complained, and turned red. He said he understood. All his life, when looked at, he had seen revulsion in people's eyes.

'I don't want to go on living,' she said. 'I want to die now, not wait for something like cancer to catch up with me.'

He said that was understandable too, though he himself wouldn't have the courage. He had read only recently, he said, in some magazine or other, that cancer was probably a virus and could be caught as easily as the common cold. If one had been in contact, that is.

'If you did have the courage,' she asked. 'How would you do it?'

'It's not something I've put my mind to,' he told her. 'Though I remember the time I had a tooth out with gas. It was a wonderful feeling, like falling from one mattress to another and every one of them filled with duck feathers. I didn't want it to stop. The dentist had to slap my face to bring me back.'

Edith Carp began to cry. He noticed that her eyes were small and carried the suggestion of a squint.

Before he went back to his own room he showed her where the key to the gas meter was hidden. 'It's always kept under the strip of lino in the cupboard,' he said. 'Most people get out their money and use it all over again. I doubt if the box has been more than half full since the thing was put in. You don't need to suffer from the cold. Mrs Darnley doesn't need the money. She's as rich as Croesus.'

He thought probably she wouldn't take advantage of the key for several days, possibly weeks. Not until her mother, if she still possessed one, had died and the room grew as cold as the grave. By then the excitement of the party would have been forgotten, the hopes of friendship dashed. All of the tenants lived very full lives and, beyond saying good morning to her as they passed her in the hall, would hardly be aware of her existence. He himself would lie low; he had done what he could.

Young Mrs Temple smelt the gas on the landing less than a week later. Edith Carp had departed some time during the night. Mrs Temple took it badly.

'We're all to blame,' she sobbed. After all, Miss Carp's was the fifth death on the second floor, not the first. They could all have done so much more, tried that bit harder to put themselves in her place, alone in London without a job, without a friend in the world.

'With the exception of you, Mr O'Malley,' Mrs Temple

amended, drying her eyes. 'You were always very good to her.'

'I did my best,' he agreed modestly. 'I don't feel I could have helped her much further.' And going into his room he put on his black tie and went out to order his usual flowers.